Drums

Drums

Brad
Henderson

Fithian Press

Santa Barbara 1997

Published by Fithian Press
A division of Daniel and Daniel, Publishers, Inc.
Post Office Box 1525
Santa Barbara, CA 93102
Orders: (800) 662-8351

Design by Karim Marouf and Eric Larson

LIBRARY OF CONGRESS CATALOGING-IN-PUBLICATION DATA
Henderson, Brad.
    Drums : a novel / by Brad Henderson.
        p. cm.
    ISBN 1-56474-207-5 (pbk. : alk. paper)
    I. Title.
  PS3558.E4824D78   1997
  813'.54—dc20   96-42226
                                                         CIP

ACKNOWLEDGEMENTS

To Dave Cowden and Alan Hodge, two drummers who challenged me and inspired me early on, when I was first learning my craft,

to John McVarish and Rob Wollenjohn, two bass players who grooved alongside me, "in the rhythm pocket," many a fine gig,

to John Rechy and James Ragan, two master writers who granted me apprenticeships,

to Dave "Hawaii Five-0" Lewis, M.D., one lone trombone player who masterminded my musical debut back in the fifth grade,

and, of course, to Fithian Press and all of its staff.

For my beloved Jessica and Re-Re

Drums

Chapter I
San Luis Obispo, California

According to L'Hôpital's Rule, if the differential functions of both numerator and denominator yield a finite quotient, then the original equation is finite itself; but ultimately, who gives a damn…?

Fall 1980

A good-sized crowd of students had gathered in the campus courtyard to watch our noon-time concert. Now, as the clocktower chimed one o'clock, we were playing the last song of the set. The single gong sounded dull and weak, almost completely masked by sharp, reedy jazz. Some listeners began to leave; most remained to listen to the finale.

Our final number was a Maynard Ferguson arrangement of "Spinning Wheel," a song popularized by Blood, Sweat and Tears. It was a good tune for the Cal Poly Jazz Group since we had a talented trumpet section that year. The arrangement was also challenging for a drummer because during the solo section there was a meter change to 6/8 time, so that the trumpet solos created a swirling, spinning sound.

We were presently in 4/4 time. I was knocking out the downbeat with my right foot. I was hitting the 2/4 upbeat on my hi-hat and snare. My right hand was "ca-chink, ca-chink, ca-chinking" a jazz ride pattern on the big cymbal. And I was happy.

My eight o'clock class that day had been "Partial Differential Equations of Physical Systems." Professor Wenzl began the lecture with a philosophical enigma: "The function F-sub-1 equal to 'x' as x goes to infinity is equal to infinity. The function F-sub-2 equal to 'e raised to the power x' as x goes to infinity is equal to infinity. Now, take the quotient of F-sub-1 over F-sub-2. Call this equation F-sub-3. Ha! Infinity racing against infinity! This, if you will, is what I call a case of quantitative Darwinism."

Dr. Wenzl paced up and down the length of the chalkboard, absently brushing against it. White dust collected on his shirt sleeves, as well as on the back of his neck where he had a habit of touching himself. He continued: "...as x approaches infinity, does the quotient of 'x' divided by 'e raised to x power' blow up? No! Calculated quite simply with L'Hôpital's Rule—it turns out to be zero, not infinity, but zero." Wenzl smiled. "Class, one must never forget the elegance of mathematics...."

Rhythm section solo. The bass player got down and played a funky riff. I stung his bass line with a matching, syncopated beat. A ripple of bass drum thuds and low-pitched notes moved lovingly in my chest.

My turn. The bass player accompanied me while I ripped out for 32 bars. I played as fast, as loud, as slick as I could. I let my arms gallop, sling energy like whips, deliver flurries of perfectly delivered blows onto centers of tom-toms, edges of cymbals. I wished my solo would last forever, but it didn't. I ended up thinking about Wenzl.

What was the difference between him and me? Why wasn't I a happy mathematician?

I, too, found math to be elegant. It was a powerfully objective discipline. The laws and postulates of math were without variance. Math problems always reduced to one definitive answer. No ambivalence. No interpretation. No opposing views. None of the subjectivism found in the Liberal Arts.

One plus one *always* equals two—yesterday, today, and tomorrow.

But in spite of all inductive reasoning, for me, I knew, right then, the elegance of math paled next to the precision, rhythm, and mastery of drums.

*   *   *

"Hey! Hey!" A frantic guy yelled at me. His voice was sharp and nervous like a polka-dotted paper horn, the kind passed out at a New Year's party.

He stood with a group of stragglers on the cement steps leading to the Student Union. I was packing up my drums. The rest of the jazz band had already left. The unnerving "Hey! Hey!" continued as he approached me, coming alone.

He wore black jeans and one of those Renaissance-type shirts with long, breezy sleeves and the breast laced up like a tennis shoe. On his feet he wore bright purple hightops. He was slight of build and had a lengthy mop of dirt-blonde hair.

"You're the drummer," he said when he reached me. "Good show, man."

"Seth Collins," he continued, "lead guitar."

"Danny Vikker," I said.

"Do you play rock 'n' roll?"

Before I could answer, one of Seth's colleagues joined us. He was also frail and earthy, and twice as peculiar. This person wore motorcycle leathers with buckles and straps, and had a toy spider dangling from a chain on his belt—a rubber tarantula as big as a rat. "I'm Spook," he said.

"Danny might be the band's next drummer," Seth said.

"What?" I said.

"Good," said Spook. "That's hhoorrrrr-ribly great."

The guitarist explained to me that he was in a local band. They needed a drummer and he was inviting me to audition.

"Are you in the group, too?" I asked Spook.

"Just a fan," he replied. "You know I wish I played the harpsichord." He petted his toy spider as if it were alive.

Seth and I exchanged phone numbers. "Gotta jam," Seth said. "We'll talk later about when and where."

I hadn't agreed to do anything, but Seth Collins acted like everything was all set.

"I have to go also," said Spook. "Peace and darkness, man."

"So long, guys."

That was how it all started.

*   *   *

After garnering a "C" on my next quiz in Wenzl's class, I called Seth.

He gave me directions to a house on the east side of town, in an old, run-down section where a lot of college students rented. When I drove to the east side, I usually took the 101 Causeway, which zips over downtown and passes by the college, but that night I opted for the slow route, the zig-zagging drive along downtown's network of tidy, perpendicular streets.

As I cruised Marsh Street, the atmosphere was festive; groups of people moved on the sidewalks, most of them traveling to and from the bars, positioned like neon oases along S.L.O.'s main drag. I passed Aces, the most popular dance bar, and heard the sound of thumping rock 'n' roll. A line of people at least a block long waited to get into the overcrowded club. I wasn't an expert on the local club scene, but I had heard people mention Seth's band. Bandit was supposed to be a hot act.

Imagining myself onstage behind a set of drums, I turned onto Johnson Street and disappeared into the east side. No more downtown bustle. Above silhouettes of boxy houses, street lights incandesced into frozen star-shapes. Everything else was lunar blue.

A Dodge van was parked in front of 29 Orchid Street just as Seth said it would be. I heard the faint sound of an electric guitar coming from somewhere inside. On the front porch there was a big wooden spool pushed on its side for a table; an unlit candle—almost completely melted into a wax puddle—stuck to the wheel-shaped top. Frayed beach chairs surrounding the spool were pushed out into a haphazard, open pattern, as though the chairs' occupants had risen suddenly and ecstatically, not looking back. The doorbell button dangled from a thick, spiraling wire. It still worked.

An Asian fellow wearing drawstring pants and a striped, sleeveless T-shirt appeared in front of me. He was lean-muscled and tall. His crisp white outfit accentuated and made especially radiant his bronze, outdoorsy skin.

"Greetings, dude," he said. "You're not nearly as ugly as Seth said you were." He smiled broadly, showing silver caps on each of his eyeteeth. "I take it you're the drummer?"

"You win the prize," I said. "I'm the drummer."

"I play bass. The name's Jay." He gave me a healthy slap on the back. "Entrée, dude." I followed behind him.

Aside from a state-of-the-art stereo and a large collection of record albums, the interior of the house was a collage of seashells, beer cans, grocery store house plants, and mismatched furniture. Typical college student living. Jay and I passed through a kitchen with a sink full of dirty pots and pans, and stepped into the "studio," previously a garage.

The studio was wired with a variety of colored flood lights, but now a bank of overhead fluorescent tubes lit the room. Sound-absorbing carpet covered the floor and walls. It had taken several different colored remnants to complete the job. A beat-up armchair, some fat pillows, and a low table occupied one corner of the room. On the table was the P.A. console; P.A. speakers hung on opposite walls. In the middle were guitar amps, keyboards, microphones on stands, and an empty space left for a set of drums.

Old promo posters were pinned to the wall carpet here and there. One poster showed an air-brushed picture of a beautiful girl with green eyes; a sexy girl with long dark hair; a spunky girl wearing a dangerously short mini-skirt and pointed, knee-high boots. Her image was done in an avant-garde smear, so that she looked as though she were in motion—singing, dancing, jumping all at the same time.

I wondered who she was.

Seth Collins sat patiently strumming his electric guitar. "Hey," he said. "Good to see you." He reached for the cigarette that was smoldering in an ashtray on top of his amp. "Hang loose. I'm in the middle of transposing a new song I want us to play tonight."

Seth motioned toward a third band member, who was bent over a disassembled keyboard, fiddling with the instrument's electrical innards. The unbolted casing lay on the floor. It was painted red, white, and blue.

"That's Uwe," Seth said. "We're 'Bandit.'"

Uwe was a blonde, Teutonic-looking fellow, with narrow shoulders and a thick waist that made his hefty body look like a tree trunk. His face had a handsome shape, but was sore-looking, pockmarked. He ignored Seth, and also Jay and me, and continued to work on his instrument.

"I told you not to buy that thing," Seth said.

"I'll have it fixed in a minute," said Uwe.

"It's junk, and it sounds like junk. You've got a decent piano and synthesizer. That old organ is a dinosaur, man."

Uwe's lips twisted up in rebellion. "There," he said. "Just a bad connection." A piercing, circus-sound blasted out of one of the amps.

"Praise the Lord, man," Jay said.

"I don't know what Seth's problem is," Uwe told me. "A frat brother let me have this thing for 100 bills."

"It would cost you $200 for him to take it back," said Seth.

Uwe ignored the guitarist. "You see," he confided to me and Jay, "I have some ideas of my own for this band. I'm the type of musician that's always looking for a new sound. The Beatles used an organ. So did the Doors."

"Whatever," Jay said.

"I'm serious," said Uwe. "I shit you not."

Jay swung open the garage door. We unloaded fiberboard cases from the back of my Toyota pickup. I broke out my set.

Seth suggested that we start with a song by the Vapors that I'd never heard of.

"Let's begin with standard fare," said Jay. "A Stones tune. Maybe some Who."

"How about 'Johnny B. Goode'?" Uwe suggested.

I nodded. Of course I knew that one.

"Going way back," Jay said.

"Way too pedestrian," said Seth.

"It's a classic," said Jay.

"Maybe we can do something creative here." Seth's expression brightened, and he showed Jay a new riff, which he hoped would spice up the old rock 'n' roll standby.

Chuck Berry would have hardly recognized the piece the way we were playing it. Seth and Jay's guitar work was aggressive and new wave. Uwe's synthesizer gave the song a space-age digital sound. Seth sang lead, and Jay sang backup vocals. Seth's singing voice was scratchy like when he talked, but he hit all his notes and sang with raw conviction.

The song required a straightforward beat, but my arms, wrists, and ankles were sluggish from tense nerves. I was having trouble getting in the groove, in total sync with the other guys.

Most importantly, I had to get in sync with the bass line; bass and drums equalled rhythm. Jay was a good bass man; he sensed I was having trouble following him, and turned so that I could watch his fingers work the fat strings. I understood the language of his hands. Bass line and drum beat meshed.

Seth left his mike and played a guitar solo in front of my drums. A serenade. *You're doing it now, Vikker*, the guitar said. *That's it.*

We drug out the piece a long time and had a lot of fun with it. But the jam persisted to be an audition. When the guys were satisfied I could play a beat, they had me do some short, four-bar solos. One of them would improvise for four bars, then I took over and filled four measures with fancy drumming.

Seth went. I went. Uwe went. I went. Now. I counted as Jay finished his solo. Three-Two-Three-Four. Four-Two-Three-Four.

I went around the tom-toms playing sixteenth notes in triplet-like patterns, punctuating the fast patterns with the bass drum.

That count was: One-Eee-And-Dah-Two-Eee-And-Dah-Three-Eee-And-Dah-Four-Eee-And-Dah…

The hand-foot pattern was: (roto-tom #1) Right-Left-Bass (roto-tom #2) Right-Left-Bass (smallest tom) Right-Left-Bass (next tom) Right-Left-Bass (big tom) Right-Left-Bass…

I was eager to play on. Musically, I hadn't done a two-and-a-half back flip with a double twist, but I felt confident: things were going okay.

There was a cassette deck wired into the P.A., and Seth put in a tape of more songs he wanted us to try with me playing drums. We listened to three tunes, one by the Police, one by the Talking Heads, and the third a dancy piece by Pat Benatar that Seth transposed earlier so he and Jay could sing it without busting their larynxes. I listened to each number several times, trying to digest the melodies and rhythmical patterns.

The audition lasted nearly four hours. We played all of the copy tunes Seth wanted us to do, then jammed on some of the band's originals.

When it was over, the band members excused themselves and went in the house to hold a conference. I waited in the studio, and listened to the dull buzz of amps permeating sweaty, wrung-out air.

The guitarist, bass man, and keyboardist said nothing when

they returned.

Jay lit up a bong. "Take a hit, dude."

I grasped the long, bamboo pipe. Jay showed me where the carburetor hole was on the side, and I placed my mouth in the circular opening on top, and drew in. I heard water bubbling in the chamber. Jay pushed my finger off the carburetor hole.

Cool, humidified smoke rushed into my lungs. It tasted like burnt pine. The volume of smoke in my lungs doubled, tripled, quadrupled.

I couldn't get oxygen. My eyes cried. I bent over with gagging coughs.

"Forgot to tell him it was expando weed," Uwe chuckled.

"Sorry," Seth said.

"You all right?" Jay asked. "You look pretty fucked up. You took way too big of a hit."

The bong went around a second time. I let it pass.

We sat in the center of the room, Indian-style on the floor. Seth, Jay, and Uwe buzzed on the pot—red-eyed, quiet.

Above us, beyond our circle, I saw the eyes of the beautiful poster girl staring sideways like the Mona Lisa. She dared me to seek an answer. She was impatient. So was I.

"Am I in?"

Seth began to explain, "We auditioned six drummers so far."

"We were supposed to give one more guy a chance after you," said Uwe.

"But us three talked. We like you pretty well," said Jay.

"We played this town for almost three years," Seth continued, "then we lost our drummer. He left us for another band in L.A." Seth scratched the stubble on his chin with his thin fingers. "Now, I guess, we've got that problem taken care of."

Jay grinned. "You're in, if you want."

I accepted. It seemed like an elegant thing to do.

"Don't forget to tell him about Abbey-baby," Uwe said,

"now that she's made her grand entrance into town again."

"Don't be such a donkey," Jay said.

"I'm just trying to make a point, that's all," said Uwe. "We've got our new drummer. We could do fine without Abbey."

Seth turned on Uwe, "She's our ticket, you idiot! People love her. She's a better musician than you'll ever be." Seth paused. "Maybe better than all of us."

Seth puffed on his cigarette to calm down. "There she is." He was pointing toward the beautiful poster girl. "I painted her a couple years ago. Do you like it?"

"She's a knock-out," I said.

"About a year after we started the band, there were some hard feelings. She left town," Seth continued.

"More like she totally disappeared," said Jay.

"She's back. We want her to sing lead again. We're doing okay without her, but with her I think we'll be able to really go someplace."

"She's stringing us along, man," said Uwe. "She hasn't said yes."

"She will," said Seth. "Give her time."

"She digs the limelight, and it digs her," said Jay. "How can she say no?"

"She can't," said Seth.

I looked once again at the promo poster of Abbey. I hoped Seth was right.

Chapter 2
Swashbuckling at Spook's

Winter Quarter

Jay phoned and said he would stop by my place around eight. Spook's party wasn't supposed to start until nine or ten, but Jay suggested that we have a few beers before heading over.

"Got to get in the proper frame of mind," Jay Wong reminded me before hanging up.

Thursday night we had played Aces and during break Seth's ghoulish friend, Spook, invited all of us to this party. Friday we had played Chee's Nightclub, and we were supposed to play again tonight, Saturday, but Uwe's frat was having an exchange with some sorority and Uwe refused to miss it.

Seth wasn't thrilled about canceling the gig. Jay and I were bummed, too, but we decided to make the most of it and go over to Spook's. Seth said he was going to lock himself in the studio and write songs.

I was still getting used to the idea of being a rock musician, and, as I got dressed for the party, putting on jeans and a button-down shirt, I wondered how I might look with a pierced ear like Jay, or with a mop of hair like Seth? After splashing on some after-shave, I examined myself in the dresser mirror. I doubted if me and my pug nose and puny chest would ever make the cover of *Rolling Stone*.

I sat down at my desk, deciding that I might as well do a homework problem or two while I waited for Jay. Ironically, the one class I thought would be winter quarter's cake-walk turned out to be winter quarter's bear. "Senior Seminar for Math Majors" was hardly a breezy, round-table discussion. The professor assigned twenty or thirty tedious problems every damn class, and the solutions weren't in the back of the book; the professor made up the exercises himself.

Gloomily, I reduced problem number twenty-four down to a messy integral—all problems in Senior Seminar invariably reduced to either a messy integral or differential. I was really getting sick of college. Sick of the whole business.

*   *   *

Earlier that day I received a phone call from my father. Dad and I did most of our serious talking on the phone—a medical doctor, Dad was a busy man.

I really preferred talking to him on the phone. I didn't like the no-nonsense-turn-your-head-and-cough expression he put on his face when he harassed me about my grades.

"Are you giving your professors a run for their money?" Dad asked in his ex-All-American tight end voice.

"I guess so," I replied.

"I hear the weather's been exceptionally blissful down there at that resort where you're going to school. Here in Sacramento, we're up to our elbows in fog. It's miserable. A lot of bronchitis going around."

"That's too bad."

"Had a few spare minutes and gave Stanford a call—on your behalf. My old alma mater. Stanford's math department is topnotch. Of course their medical school is better."

"I know. I know."

"Someone's application was not on file."

"I've been sort of busy."

"Yes?"

"Playing drums."

"Christ almighty, you sound like some hippie person from the sixties."

"Dad, I've been thinking—"

"What the hell is it this time, Danny. Still a loner? Still depressed because you left behind all your high school friends? I told you to join a fraternity. A good way to network. Crap! You could finally do something, son, if you'd get off your butt and mail in those applications. I say crap!"

"Screw you, Dad," I yelled into the receiver.

But Dad had already hung up. I didn't have the guts to tell him anything like that to his face.

*   *   *

Jay arrived.

"I hate to tell you this, dude, but you stink," he said. "Didn't your mother ever tell you that ladies prefer the natural aroma of a man?"

I sniffed the air and realized I had applied my after-shave a bit thick. "Screw you," I said.

"Screw yourself, donkey."

Jay was obviously feeling punk. He had threaded a safety pin through the hole in his ear lobe. The black button pinned to the breast of his Sex-Wax T-shirt read in orange, brush-stroked letters, "Abbey Butler and Bandit!!!"

Jay, like Seth, still seemed convinced that their elusive ex-singer was going to be with us again soon. I hadn't seen hide nor hair of her.

"Dude, I had such a day," Jay exclaimed. "The waves off Morro Rock were breaking perfect. Cold as a witch's tit, but, fuck it, I surfed the big blue till dusk."

"I spent the day doing homework. I'm still not done."

"Bummer.

"School's a drag," Jay said. "That's why I blew it off for a while. I just take people's money down at the record shop and listen to good tunes. When the waves are good, the boss lets me skate." Jay's eyes squinted sleepily as he preached about the good life.

Sometimes Jay was so content it made me a little sick.

"You want to spin an album?" I asked, pointing to my stereo.

Jay selected *Reggatta de Blanc* by the Police. He took the album out of the jacket then put it on the turntable. He applied the disc cleaning brush before letting the stylus drop onto the first track.

Sting's cutting voice rang out the words to "Message in a Bottle" as I went to the fridge for brews. We drank a six-pack.

*   *   *

Spook, as it turned out, lived in a rented house not far from my apartment in the Arroyo Lake suburb. It was a pleasant West Coast winter night, but Jay insisted that we drive rather than walk.

"When I leave the party with some gorgeous babe," Jay said, "I want to have some wheels right there."

Jay's statement sounded overly macho and I laughed. "Seriously," he continued, "let's cruise in the van. I don't like to walk when I'm wasted."

The old Dodge engine didn't have enough power to squeal the tires. As Jay lay on the gas pedal, the big van reared up in front like a giant rocking horse, and I was pushed back into my seat. We let out crazy whoops and yells as Jay accelerated past the speed limit.

We ran out of breath. We stopped shouting.

I listened to Jay's grinding downshifts of the engine. "Don't want to get popped for a 502," he muttered.

We inched along about 25 mph. We seemed to be stuck in time. I wanted to keep racing.

More and more, I didn't like moments of stasis. When I had them, there was this holier than thou part of me that, given nothing else to do, dwelled on school, made me feel guilty, said I oughta buckle down, thought my father was right.

Yet there was another part of me that thought he was wrong. Piss on him. Piss on Wenzl. Piss on Senior Seminar in Math. This was the part of me that liked to play drums. This was the part of me that liked to keep moving, keep in rhythm with the here and now. This was a part of myself that was relatively new.

"Can't you go any faster?" I asked Jay.

"We're here," he said.

I saw a house with jack-o'-lanterns in the windows. Cars everywhere parked on the street—some on the front lawn.

Spook greeted us at the front door.

"Hello," I said.

"The pumpkins are bitchin'," said Jay, "just like Halloween."

Our host was in his glory, wearing a sweatshirt with the green face of Frankenstein on front and the brown jowls and white fangs of the Wolfman on back. He wore his black hair greased back, and had powdered his already pale skin death-white. From the neck up, Spook looked like Dracula, until he opened his mouth. His teeth were small, yellowish, and uneven—not big, white, and sharp.

We passed a darkly lit room filled with people dancing. None of the other guests wore costumes like Spook, but many were unusual looking. I watched with fascination as a red-haired young man weighing about 300 pounds did blobbish somersaults across the middle of the dance floor. The dancers screamed with joy and jumped out of his way. "That's Big Ben. He's one of my roommates," said Spook.

Through an aqua-black sliding glass door, I caught a glimpse of the backyard. I saw human silhouettes and amber glows that hovered like fireflies, joints and cigarettes holding the silhouettes together in clusters.

We passed through the kitchen, the only room with bright light. Spook side-stepped the line to the keg and drew Jay and me two icy beers. We declined the hors d'oeuvres—a huge bowl of chips, beside it a smaller bowl of haphazardly concocted guacamole, with bits and pieces of avocado skin included.

The room we ended up in had Spook written all over it. Eerie posters decorated the walls, and collections of plastic monster models were showcased on onyx black shelves. Jay pointed out a miniature guillotine that chopped the head off a little plastic man.

"It works," Spook told us.

There were also textbooks, several bookcases of them. Many of them I recognized as required reading for science courses: *Biology of Humans, Tipler's Physics, Advanced Biochemistry.* Above a small, organized desk, I spied a row of certificates. One was a Dean's List award, bearing the name of its recipient, "Melvin Stevenson, Jr."

Spook, a.k.a. Melvin, asked Jay to lock the door. He unfolded a triangular piece of paper, revealing a small pile of white powder and white crystalline mixed together. He let the mixture spill onto a mirror.

"Look at those outrageous rocks," Jay said soberly, his eyes transfixed to the glass.

Cocaine. I had only smoked pot once before joining Bandit. Now I got high at least a couple times a week. Getting stoned after practice was a part of our ritual. But this seemed more serious.

The laws against cocaine were more strict, and you were up shit creek if you got caught with it. Also, the news was always reporting someone dying from it. Too potent.

I didn't want any. Q.E.D.

As the party boomed beyond these walls, Spook used a razor blade to chop white grains until they were dust; then he cut out three smaller piles from the large one. He said, "Some for me, some for Jay, some for Dan."

"We can get some hefty snorts out of those. Thanks, man." Jay's voice was both polite and rushed. He was ready.

Spook made the three piles into twelve long, thin lines. He stuck one end of a short straw up his nostril and bent over the mirror so the other end of the straw could vacuum some powder. He changed nostrils and repeated this ritual. His eyes watering, he passed the straw to me.

"I'll pass," I said.

"Are you crazy?" Jay said. "There's about a hundred bucks worth of blow here. Take it when you can get it, dude."

"You go ahead." I handed him the straw.

Jay rid the mirror of his share very quickly. Then he started eyeing mine. "What do you say, Spook—two and two?"

"Yeah sure," answered Spook.

"Danny's a math major," Jay explained to our host. "He's cool, but he's kind of straight."

"I'm pre-med," said Spook, rather ho-hum. "Go on, Jay. You first."

Before Jay got the straw up his nose, I reclaimed it. Gotta keep moving.

"Maybe you and my father could get together sometime," I said to Spook.

Private joke. He didn't get it.

I inhaled.

High in my nasal passages the substance gathered and then dripped onto the back of my throat. The taste of the substance was antiseptic, yet good—indescribable, really, in terms of other flavors and smells.

The first sensation came on fast. My gums became numb as if from novocaine. My lips hung open loosely.

The second sensation hit soon after: everything seemed so suddenly Right: everything was so crystalline like those white rocks.

In the room of textbooks and plastic creatures, Spook, Jay, and I bobbed our heads to bassy reverberations. We buzzed.

"Good stuff," Jay complimented Spook, who was bug-eyed

and fooling around with a small, green model of a lizard-monster. Spook let out a disconcerting roar.

I sniffed casually like Jay kept doing.

Someone pounded on the door from outside in the hall.

"The cops are here," said a female voice. The knocking continued. "What are you doing in there? Come on, Spook, everybody's scared."

An entire liter of adrenalin shot straight into my heart. I felt sweaty, dazed, weak. "Shit," I said. "Hide that stuff, Spook."

Spook slid the mirror under his bed. "Bummer," he said.

Again the voice sounded from behind the door, "What should we do, Spook? The cops want to talk to the person in charge. They want to check I.D.s." The voice paused. "God, Spook, they want to bust us."

Clipped images of jail cells and rusty iron bars flashed in and out of focus. I saw Jay pacing the room like a nervous zoo cat.

Two girls bowled over Spook as he unlatched the door. Another liter of adrenalin flowed into my chest. This time there was not enough room and some flowed directly into my brain. Straight adrenalin into my brain. It made me queasy. The girls crashed into Jay and me.

Our bodies tangled as we fell to the floor. No one spoke.

The girls erupted with giggles. One of them pranced over and slammed shut the door, trapping all five of us in Spook's room. "Geeezzz," she said, "we thought you guys were never going to open up." Her face had a hard, sexy edge.

"Were you guys scared?" asked her friend, who was slight and twiggy, and wearing a lot of blue eye shadow.

Spook was not the least bit ruffled. "This is Jane, and this is Leslie. My two other roommates." Jane was the cute, petite girl and Leslie was the rough, ravenous girl, who asked us to call her Flipper. I'd seen them before with Spook at one of our gigs.

"You know what I want?" Flipper asked.

"I can't imagine," Spook said.

"Come on, Spooky," Jane said. "Where is it?"

"We did it all," Spook replied.

"That's shitty," Flipper said. "You're not being nice to your two girls." She playfully shook her finger at Spook. Spook seemed on the verge of letting out a giant yawn.

He recovered his mirror, and all of us gathered around it. Jane sat next to me; Flipper sat next to Jay; Spook sat by himself. This arrangement pleased our host.

The girls hungrily snorted white powder, and the rest of us did some more lines as well. Spook said he had to get back to his party. As he left, he winked at me. It was a funny wink. He had a hard time holding one eye open while closing the other— it was more of a contorted squint.

"So," I said to the girls. "This is some party."

"Yeah, so it is," Jay said.

"So what?" teased Flipper.

Jane pinched me lightly on the stomach. "So there," she said.

"You know what?" Flipper said. "You guys are a great band. Jane and I saw you at Aces."

"I like drummers," added Jane, who kept staring at me with her blue butterfly eyes.

"I like bass players," announced Flipper.

Flipper hopped onto Jay's lap. Jay couldn't seem to stop grinning. "Bitchin'," he said.

The cocaine screamed in my head like a high-pitched noise.

Jay and Flipper played with Spook's toys. Jay raised the blade of the miniature guillotine and let it fall and chop off the little plastic man's head. The head dropped into a little plastic bucket. Jay tugged the guide string and hauled up the blade, revealing a little plastic neck-stub painted red.

"Gross!" exclaimed Flipper. "Spook is so weird."

"I think Spook is a pretty cool dude," Jay said.

He and Flipper were hitting it off. I couldn't think of

anything to say to Jane. She kept staring at me with her blue butterfly eyes.

"Let's go dance," I said finally.

We made our way through the halls, through the cocktail darkness, dark-orange and purplish-blue. I felt like I had a fever and my skin prickled. My arm was around Jane. Paranoia nipped at me. Taking cocaine, Danny?! Crap!! Pathetic loser!!

I kept moving. I willed myself to blend into the noise and the frenzy, like lotion into skin.

I led Jane into the dancing. I liked to dance. It felt like I was playing drums with my body.

She had a good sense of rhythm. I wished for a slow song. Instead the electric music made us twist and jump.

We danced for five or six numbers. The music was exceedingly loud. I grasped her small shoulders and spoke directly into one of her ears. "Take a break?" I asked.

"Sure," she said.

We went outside and stood in the cool, dark quiet. I liked Jane and fantasized about her and me making love. Yet, once again, our conversation had stalled. That is, until she mentioned Domino.

"You're not at all like he was," she said.

"What?"

"Domino. The band's old drummer."

"You knew him?" I asked. Seth, Jay, and Uwe never discussed Bandit's former drummer.

"Sure, everyone knew *him*," Jane said.

I asked her why I was so different.

"I don't know exactly," she replied. "For one thing, he was so show-biz."

"What?"

"You're more quiet. I like that. Domino used to get so obnoxious when he partied." She paused. "Not like a jock or that type—. He didn't stomp around and break stuff. He just got real braggy."

"I see."

"He was full of a lot of B.S."

"When I joined Bandit, all the others told me was that the last drummer quit because he got a better offer."

"Yeah—that and because of him and Abbey," Jane said, "because they broke up."

I'd never met Domino or Abbey. But, nevertheless, Jane's words skewered my gut. These two. Their legacy. I wanted to know everything.

But this is what I said: "I guess that's their business."

"Oh it's no secret Domino and Abbey were lovey-dovey," Jane said. "Then they had a fight and Abbey left the band. Domino and the rest of the guys kept playing and they did okay for a while."

Jane recklessly crossed her twiggy arms and cast a look of reproach. "Abbey's a bitch anyway, even if she is a great singer. You know, I heard Seth wants to let her back in. Maybe he likes her, too. What do you know?"

"Only gossip," I said.

As Jane had the strange habit of doing, she reached out and pinched my stomach. "I like it that you're in the band now."

I should have stopped on that encouraging note. "So," I asked rather smugly, "was this Domino a decent drummer?"

"Most people say he's the best drummer they've ever heard. I bet he gets in a really good band down in L.A." Jane's blue butterfly eyes became apologetic. "Let's do some more toot."

I followed her back to Spook's room and we located the mirror under the bed. Quickly she shoved the mirror in front of me and motioned for me to make us some lines, which I did as best I could. She sucked up two long ones. I did the same, and soon became full of that clear, perfect high I felt earlier. I was having fun again.

We each did another, and another. We hummed and

twitched and sniffed through our nostrils. The medicinal energy that had previously sparkled my thoughts and made all sensation seem so Right and shiny, now centralized into one, single, urgent drive to make it with Jane.

I also felt disoriented, anxious, and shy.

She changed that. "I'm so hot," she said, her voice low and amorous. "Let's go to my room and get naked."

We made love furiously. Jane still had her top on, and I had my pants around my ankles in an awkward wad. We rested and then finished undressing and climbed under her sheets. We did it again—this time more slowly and proficiently. Then we lay there, both awake.

The sweat and friction between our bodies dissolved most of Jane's makeup. Her blue butterfly eyes were gone. This young woman, whose face was so near I could feel her warm, humid exhales, seemed naggingly, naggingly foreign.

*   *   *

It took a moment to place where I was. I did not move. I did not want to wake the girl. I needed to think, alone.

Fragmented voices played in my mind: "Domino…So show-biz…She disappeared…Cocaine…Crap…You loser."

My nostrils were dry and my mouth tasted like chalk. I lay there feeling the presence of a naked stranger beside me, hearing the crisp hum of morning; when I played these sensations against flashbacks of the night it all seemed incongruent. I wanted to get out of Jane's bed and out of her, Spook, and that other girl's house.

I met Jay in the hallway. He had the same thing in mind. "Getting the hell out of Dodge?" I whispered.

"Breakfast with Flipper is something I don't want to experience," he said. "She's into some pretty weird stuff."

"Oh?"

"She wanted me to tie her up and shit like that." The

corners of Jay's mouth turned down. "She was on the rag, too."

"Marvelous," I said.

Jay put his finger to his lips. "Sssshhh," he said.

Inside the van, the compartment was cold and damp with the morning. "So how come you bailed?" Jay asked. "Jane seemed pretty cool."

I didn't answer. Instead, I asked him a question. "Did your old drummer really used to go out with Abbey?"

"Yeah," he replied. He took a long time before he reached down and turned the key in the ignition. "But I guess, Danny, that's like all water under the bridge." Jay looked straight ahead as he drove, and made it a point to leave it at that.

Chapter 3
Making the Rudiments Sound as They Are

My first music teacher's name was Mr. Luck. He was a peculiar, thin, high-strung man with crooked and aged teeth. The thick, black vinyl frames of his eyeglasses were faded from the whiteness of sweat. The name "Luck" had no significance for me as a fifth grade kid. Now, however, it seems like the perfect antonym for what Meriam Luck had none of. There were five elementary schools in the Sacramento suburb where I grew up, and Mr. Luck was assigned to drive from institution to institution in his "music center on wheels," a moth-balled school bus. The old bus was painted gray and all the bench seats were removed; in their place were racks for the band instruments that Mr. Luck loaned to his students. Along the right-hand side of the bus, underneath a bank of square, filmy windows, was a long counter hedged with metal stools. It was there I learned to play the snare drum.

Once a week I got to leave class, in order to visit Mr. Luck in the school parking lot for a lesson. He screamed from beginning to end.

"Didn't I tell you not to put your drumsticks together with rubberbands? You're going to wreck the finish on them. Rubberbands cause *oxidation* marks," he ranted when I arrived.

If he would have told me what oxidation meant, and if two drumsticks bound together by a rubberband didn't make such a good mock airplane propeller when one stick was wound against the other, I probably would have listened, but back then

I nodded dumbly and mumbled, "Yes, Mr. Luck, I was just trying to keep 'em together so I wouldn't lose 'em."

"Get those wrists warmed up," he blurted next.

Upon command I placed a drumstick in each hand, gripping the centers of the sticks as if they were batons. I rotated my wrists back and forth, back and forth. That exercise is one I never forgot. It was a cool thing to do; while brass players got their mouth pieces warm by sucking on them like metal lollipops, and woodwinds started first by slobbering over their reeds, drummers merely twirled their sticks and yawned. Later, when I progressed to playing a drum set in a group, I still waited out the moments before a gig with that same routine I learned from Meriam Luck.

"How's that roll coming?" Mr. Luck would inquire. "Okay, begin. right-Right, left-Left, right-Right, left-Left. No. No. Start again. Your sticks aren't in proper position. The angle's wrong—too close to the rim. When I want a rim shot, by God, I'll ask for one. right-Right, left-Left, right-Right, left-Left. No. No. Accent the second sticking. Better. Better. right-*Right*, left-*Left*, right-*Right*, left-*Left*...."

In a couple minutes I would be buzzing out a choppy long roll. *Bbbzzzzzzzzzzzz*. At these times, Mr. Luck would grin his dirty, crooked grin, and I would grin back.

But these momentary calms were short-lasted. "Now back down. Slow it up. No. No. Not so fast. Control. Use a little control." Soon we'd be back to, "right-Right, left-Left, right-Right, left-Left." Ten minutes into my lesson I felt as much a nervous wreck as he.

Mr. Luck taught me how to play a paradiddle, flam, a five, seven, and nine stroke roll, and, of course, the infamous long roll, upon which he placed so much weight.

"Danny," he would lecture, "first, you have to learn the rudiments. One must always start out with the rudiments. They develop a drummer's speed and coordination, and *all* drum playing is built upon them."

"Vikker," he called me by my last name when he was most serious, "do you know how the rudiments got their names?"

"Not really, Mr. Luck," I would say politely.

"Back in the old days, back when drummers marched with the armies, the art of snare drumming was passed from one drummer to the next by word of mouth. Each rudiment derived its name simply from how it sounded.

"Play 'right-left-right-right, left-right-left-left.' Quickly now. Quickly.

"Now say, 'paradiddle, paradiddle.'"

"Paradiddle, paradiddle."

"You see what I mean, Vikker?"

Mr. Luck loved that story. He told it to me often. "Rrrrooolll. Rrrrooolll. Fla-aamm. Fla-aamm. Paradiddle. Paradiddle," he impressed upon me. "Rudiments are the beginning. Rudiments sound as they are."

*   *   *

When the two girls and Jay arrived at 29 Orchid Street, I was sitting in front of the stereo with Seth and Uwe, listening to Pete Townshend's *Empty Glass* album. There were a couple of songs on the record that Seth felt Bandit ought to try. Seth was putting together a new repertoire, or list—four collections of songs—sets A, B, C, and D—that each took an hour to play; four hours worth of music was enough material for a typical gig. About a quarter of the songs were originals, and the rest were copy tunes, borrowed from popular, bigname bands. Seth hoped eventually we would have enough originals so that we didn't have to rely on copy tunes.

"What took you so long?" Seth asked the three persons who spilled into the house. He was excited. Tonight was our first practice with the band's former lead singer.

"I was starved, man," Jay said. "We stopped at the Dark

Room for some chow."

Jay wore Hawaiian-print Bermuda shorts, an unbuttoned peacoat, and rubber thongs. Exposure to the brisk night air gave the brown skin on Jay's face and bare legs a pinkish hue.

The two girls were sharing a dish of frozen yogurt. Abbey, whom I immediately recognized from Seth's painting, took the plastic spoon from her girlfriend's hand and placed a large carob-coated scoop in her mouth. "Care for a taste?" she teased Seth.

Seth didn't reply. He lit a smoke and gave one to Abbey, then lit another match with a quick, deft strike and put an amber glow on the end of her cigarette.

Abbey and Jay continued to kid around with Seth. Abbey's friend didn't seem to mind not being included in the conversation. She ate her frozen yogurt happily, and didn't offer any to me or Uwe.

After a while, the guitarist, bass player, and songstress stopped chatting, and Abbey Butler stared at me with penetrating green eyes.

She wore an unusual array of color and fashion on her slim, curvy body. A black and white checkered sportjacket draped her square, confident shoulders, and flowed down her torso with streamy, cosmopolitan lines. The lapels of the oversized man's jacket flopped loosely; a necktie dangled well past her waist and was tied with a funny girlish knot. She wore tight blue-green slacks, high heel boots, and feathered earrings. As she removed her gaze from me to wink saucily at Seth and Jay, the weightless earrings brushed her smooth neck like naughty angels.

Her stare returned. "Well—," she said, "aren't you going to introduce yourself? The boys told me they found a new drummer. I'm not blind."

"Cut the theatrics, Abbey," said Seth.

"Oh shush," Abbey said pertly. She returned to me. "Seth always tries to be so level-headed. You know what I think?" Her green eyes swam over me like a screaming gust of hot wind. "He ought to try letting go. It's really fun. I do it all the time."

"I'm Danny," I said. "I—"

"They told me your name," she said, cutting me off, as though I were being excessively dull. "I'm Abbey, of course. We already know that, don't we? The point is that we've never *met*—in flesh and blood. Now we have. Savvy?"

I nodded. The physical space between me and the capricious girl vanished. It felt as though her sharp, painted fingernails were tapping on my chest. She was ten times more beautiful in person than she was in Seth's painting.

"They say you play drums well," Abbey continued. "I hope so. Seth and I mean business this year. Oh, I'm sorry—." She stopped and looked at Jay as if to acknowledge that he was a part of the plan, too, then she looked at Uwe more superficially.

Uwe said, "I knew she was going to do this if we let her back in."

"Do what?" Seth asked.

"Do what?" Abbey repeated.

"She's already taking over the whole show," Uwe said.

"Mellow out," Jay said.

Abbey said, "Isn't a lead singer supposed to steal the show, or something like that?"

"Yes," Uwe said.

"Then what's your problem?" Seth asked.

"Nothing," Uwe said.

Uwe did have a problem. Abbey didn't like him. That was obvious.

Abbey's friend was still finishing her frozen yogurt, daintily spooning the last bit from the bottom of a pink plastic dish. "Hi," she said demurely. "I think it's nice the band has a new drummer."

Abbey announced, "This is Zoe Cleopatra Hash. Isn't that a beautiful name?"

"Yes, it is," I said cautiously. "Very beautiful, and very different."

"Oh my," Zoe replied.

"Zoe and I are spiritual sisters," said Abbey. "We live together. We talk about everything. And we get in all sorts of trouble—that is, when I'm not singing and Zoe's not studying."

The two girls batted eyes back and forth, communicating some sort of secret message. Abbey grabbed Zoe by the hand and led her to where the rest of us were in the living room. It was cute the way Zoe's short blonde hair bounced up and down when she moved. Like her friend's, Zoe's attire was unique. Her nautical blouse had a flapping collar and a sail boat monogrammed on the breast. She was taller than Abbey, and had long, tan legs under her jean skirt. Zoe Cleopatra Hash definitely had a subtle beauty, but next to Abbey she was no competition.

Uwe got up off the couch. Abbey and Zoe started to sit down in his place. "Don't you think we should start practice?" Uwe said. The Pete Townshend album had stopped playing on the stereo, and the speakers were making a popping noise. Uwe walked over to the stereo and flicked a switch on the turntable and ended the tone arm's lonely spiraling in the record album's center return track. Power off, the record platter stalled and greedily ate momentum in a dying spin.

"Uwe's right," Abbey said. "Let's start. I can't wait to sing."

Uwe looked rather shocked that she agreed with him.

We went into the small studio and took our places. Zoe's actions were as well-rehearsed as Jay and Seth's ritualistic guitar tuning. She homed-in on the big, tattered chair in front of the sound board and plopped herself on it, then reached over and hit the P.A.'s power switch and twirled a few knobs.

"Thanks," Seth called, as he helped Abbey with her microphone.

Zoe smiled at the guitarist and singer, then pulled a yellow felt pen and a book entitled *The History of the Mideast* out of her cloth handbag. Sitting cross-legged, her back straight and poised, she put on a pair of professorial-looking glasses and began her studies. She read diligently, high-lighting important facts with her marker. She seemed content and happy. I wondered if she had a good pair of earplugs.

"One, two, three," Seth said into his mike.

"Three, two, one," Jay said into another.

Abbey stood in the center of the room. "Test. Test. Ditto. Mine's working fine, too."

Seth stepped on one of the many foot switches in front of his amp, and the bank of overhead fluorescent lights popped off and gave way to dimmer mood lights which bled thick theatrical color; in unison, Zoe flipped on a small lamp next to the chair. Except for Zoe's pale yellow reading light, the atmosphere of the studio was a blue and red dream-vision. My eyes were on Abbey. One cheek bathed with the color of ice, the other radiating fire.

She removed her jacket and laid it swiftly at the base of her mike stand. She unbuttoned the sleeves of her blouse and tugged them up her thin forearms, leaving the sleeves ruffled and ready for work; then she arched her back and recentered her hips with a spunky snap. Last of all, Abbey shook her long brown hair, and let it fan out, wild. "It feels so wonderful to be in front of a mike again," she said. "To be with Bandit."

Abbey looked at Seth. "Shall we jam?" she asked.

"Okay, Danny," Seth said, "you start us. Here's the tempo I want: 1, 2, 3, 4."

As we fooled around and got the instruments warmed up, Abbey swayed with the music and played a tambourine. Soon she walked over to the keyboards and whispered something into Uwe's ear. He returned a sour look. She leaned over and coaxed him a second time. Uwe got up and Abbey replaced him at the keyboards. Without a glitch made in our sound, Abbey joined in playing the right chords, following the improvisation with good instinct and style. Even more energetically, she played and swayed from side to side.

We ended the jam, and Uwe happily resumed his spot on the keyboards. Seth scanned our new song list taped to his amp, and picked a song for us to try.

Then for the first time I heard Abbey sing, and as she began, even Zoe looked up from the pages of *The History of the Mideast*. As Abbey's voice delivered its first few notes of the evening, everyone, it seemed, shot me proud, welcoming signals. *Here is the voice of Bandit,* they said. *Listen to her, Danny. Now you know the secret behind Bandit is Abbey Butler.*

*   *   *

Jay Wong sat behind the cash register of "The Den," or used albums and paraphernalia department, in Jetstream Records. There were several customers browsing in Jay's area, flipping through alphabetized rows of thin, cardboard sheaths containing music magically pressed into vinyl. I didn't have any extra cash for an album, even for one of Jetstream's famous recycled records, but as I was driving home from class, I had an urge to see Jay.

"Can I help you, sir?" Jay asked, his voice earnest and professional. Then he let on that he recognized me, raised his eyebrows, and let out a robust laugh. "Hey, Danny-dude, nice of you to stop by. Pretty intense to see ole Jay in the work element, huh?"

"A little," I said.

A short, gate-like door swung open. "Come on back," he said. "Make yourself at home. Maybe you can help me sell some teeny bopper chick a fuckin' Barry Manilow button?" He shot me a wise smile, the kind in which he strained his cheeks and exposed the silver caps on his eyeteeth.

A young boy appeared before the counter. "How much are

those KISS posters, Mister?" he asked.

"Six bucks," Jay said.

"How come so much?" The kid was pudgy and had a squeaky, pre-adolescent voice.

Jay pointed to the poster of the bass player, dressed in black leather and iron and surrounded by a ring of fire and smoke. Face painted and his tongue flicking like a snake, the heavy-metal rocker looked both like a demon and a clown. "That's true art," Jay said. "It takes money to make a bitchin' picture like that. So you want it, or what?"

"I think so," the boy said.

"I'd buy it now," Jay advised. "I've been selling a lot of those. The stock's runnin' low."

The kid greedily bought four absurd-looking posters, one of each member of KISS.

After the boy left I said, "His mother's liable to come in here and make you eat those."

"I doubt it," Jay replied. "He could be doing worse stuff than collecting that junk." Jay paused. "Maybe it does the kid good? Maybe he'll end up to be *cool* and play in a band."

"You should have sent him across the street to buy some drums or a guitar."

"Whatever, dude," Jay said. "When I was his age, I owned 113 rock 'n' roll posters, and ten of them were autographed."

"Oh," I said. "What's up for tonight?"

It was Friday, and I was looking for something to do instead of study. Saturday night we all had plans. Bandit would be doing its debut gig with Abbey back on vocals.

Jay didn't answer. He was changing the "Now Playing" album, putting on some reggae. "Dig this," he said.

I preferred straightforward rock 'n' roll. Punk music was all right. Jazz was great. A little Mozart once in a while was nice, too, even if classical percussion was a bore. But I just couldn't get into reggae.

Jay said, "Not much happenin' downtown. The groups that are booked tonight suck."

"Too bad."

"Just wait until tomorrow. We'll spark things up."

Jay turned around and adjusted the volume of his reggae music so that it was even louder. It seemed like a mild earthquake was going on in the shop. "I'm going to stay home tonight. There's some good movies on the tube. Abbey and Zoe are coming over."

"Do you and one of the girls have something going on?" I asked, jealous.

"Nah," he said, "we're just good friends."

"Yeah, that's how I thought it was," I said, trying to sound nonchalant.

"The girls are a lot of fun, but they're both on some weird head trips, especially Abbey. Don't ever get on her bad side."

"I don't plan to."

He looked at me squarely. "That's good. Just because she's beautiful doesn't mean she isn't *dangerous*. Keep that in mind, dude."

A part of me appreciated that Jay was trying to give me some advice; another part of me didn't plan on paying any attention to it.

"They asked me if you were coming over, but I thought you had a jazz band gig."

"There's a gig all right, but I'm not with them anymore. Just quit. I decided one band is enough."

I had played with the Cal Poly Jazz Group for three years. The jazz band director was shocked when I told him I was quitting his group to devote all my musical energy to a rock band.

"A person has to make sacrifices."

"Exactly." I had sort of hoped Jay would think my leaving the jazz band was a big deal, but it didn't seem to faze him.

"If Stranglehold wasn't busy, we could've practiced tonight.

It's cool, I guess. Frat stuff."

"Who are you talking about?"

"Uwe, you donkey."

"Strangle—?"

"Nobody's told you about that?"

"No," I said.

Jay turned down the reggae music so that we could talk without having to scream. "Check this out man:

"When Uwe first joined the band, he was living in the dorms, and he hated his roommate. They fought about everything and liked to do things to bug each other. One time Uwe went away for the weekend and his roommate rifled through all of Uwe's stuff and stole some money. When Uwe got back he, like, went berserk and started choking the guy—till the guy passed out. A bunch of people had to pull Uwe off. He got in big trouble, man. They kicked him out of the dorms— almost out of school.

"You know that old Ted Nugent song, 'Stranglehold'?" Jay continued. "One time Seth and I jammed on it in front of him—you know, to burn him a little. It pissed him off royally. He freaked, it was scary.

"Anyway, we still call him that when he's not around. That fuckin' donkey!"

"I think I get the drift," I said.

"I probably shouldn't have brought it up."

"I get the drift," I repeated. I stroked my neck and smiled.

Jay didn't think the gesture was very funny. "Uwe's not so bad," he said. "He's loyal to the band, an original member, and most of the time he plays pretty well." Jay's voice grew more serious. "Personalities, dude. That's one of the things that gives Bandit *personality*."

A customer approached the counter with a stack of record albums. Jay typed numbers into the cash register rhythmically, like he was playing bass.

*　　*　　*

All of us sat bug-eyed and stoned in the living room of 29 Orchid Street, tripping out on the Friday Night Special TV movie, *The Wizard of Oz*. Even Seth—who was more interested in quietly strumming the Martin acoustic guitar in his lap than watching the land of Oz—now kept his eyes glued on the television with Abbey, Zoe, Jay, and me.

"The shoes, my pretty!" the Wicked Witch of the West cackled at Dorothy and her dog, Toto, who were desperately trapped in a gray, creepy castle after being captured by the hag's henchmen, the evil flying monkeys. Again, the witch mocked poor Dorothy with a shrill, wilting laugh, and taunted the farm girl heroine with long, bony, wavering green fingers. "The shoes, my pretty! The shoes!"

Unable to make the girl yield, the infuriated witch sentenced Dorothy to die and flipped over the hourglass, giving the girl until the sand ran out. The witch's pointy chin quivered as she screamed with delight. The sand was falling, falling. Then it was....

"I can't stand it," said Abbey.

"Me neither," said Zoe.

Slumped over in the corner of the living room, Seth softly strummed his Martin acoustic guitar. The girls were sitting back to back in the middle of the saggy couch. Jay and I sat on each end of the couch. Abbey rested her feet on my lap, and Zoe had her feet on Jay's. I was in seventh heaven.

The movie panned to the Lion, Tinman, and Scarecrow, scaling the witch's mountain as they followed Toto to the rescue.

"There's my buddy again," Jay said. "And I'll rrrufff! And I'll rrrufff!" Jay acted twelve years old each time he saw the Cowardly Lion. "This movie is bitchin'."

I reached down and squeezed Abbey's bare foot, which was wiggling nervously in my lap. "Chop," I said. "Chop goes the witch's guillotine on fair Dorothy's neck."

Jay filled the room with boogie man sounds.

"You guys are so full of it," Abbey said.

Seth, who hadn't said anything for a long time, agreed. "You guys are so full of shit it's leaking out your ears."

The movie cut. The television announced that the uninterrupted conclusion of *The Wizard of Oz* would follow a commercial break.

"Popcorn?" Zoe asked, going around from person to person. Jay passed out more frosty bottled beers. We'd bought a case of unrefrigerated Brand-X lager on sale. The beer tasted better now that it wasn't lukewarm.

The commercials seemed like they would never end. Toothpaste. Motor oil. Soap. Insurance. A rosy-cheeked female athlete praised a new brand of tampons on the screen. Jay chuckled. Abbey took her seat and grabbed my chin. She centered my stare into hers. "Look into my eyes," she told me. "Have you ever done this? The first person who blinks loses."

"What does the winner get?" I asked.

"Nothing," she replied. "It's only a game."

Our faces less than a foot apart, Abbey's mouth and eyes were bigger and even more consuming. I smelled her body more strongly, the rich scent of herbal perfume and traces of clove cigarettes.

"Keep looking directly into my eyes," she commanded. "Focus eye to eye."

I saw whiteness fragile as fish skin. I saw bands of multicolor, the many fragments of different shades of green, yellow, and brown—glistening like rocks underneath mountain water. I saw dark, living lenses. I knew they were looking back at me, yet my visual penetration stopped abruptly on the lens' round, wet slopes. I could not see into her mind. My eyes had gotten very dry. I blinked.

"I won," she said.

She slapped me playfully on the cheek. "Wake up," she said.

My cheek stung.

After *The Wizard of Oz*, the girls hung around some more and we watched the *Tonight Show*. As soon as Johnny Carson bid his guests good night, the girls said it was also time for them to go.

Abbey and Zoe didn't have a car. Jay had picked them up at their apartment and given them a ride over to his and Seth's place.

Abbey went into the kitchen to get her purse, and I followed her. She didn't notice me behind her until she turned around and started back into the other room. "You scared me," she said.

"You want me to give you and Zoe a ride home?" I asked.

"No, you don't need to," she said.

"Why not?" I asked.

"Because Jay can drive us," she replied. "You don't have to."

"It's easier for me," I said. "Jay will have to make a special trip. I have to drive myself home anyway."

Abbey gave me a resigned look. She started to walk off, but stopped. She put her purse back on the counter.

"Do you think I look like Judy Garland?" she asked.

I wanted to say something clever. But Abbey didn't look at all like Judy Garland to me.

When I said nothing, she said, "I guess I don't."

I thought for a minute. "I'll tell you who you look like. You look like Marilyn Monroe."

"A blonde?" Abbey said incredulously. "My hair is brown."

"I mean you're pretty like her."

"Oh, I see."

She picked up her purse and searched inside of it. She pulled out a makeup pencil and drilled it against her face. She did this so quickly I didn't know what she was doing. When she removed her hand, I saw a perfect mole on her cheek. "Do you like it?" she asked.

"Sure," I said. When she did impetuous little things like

that it drove me nuts.

She took out a mirror and inspected her work. "Yes," she said. "I like it, too." She looked at herself some more in her compact, using the small mirror to compare one cheek with the other. "I should get Zoe. We have to go."

"I had fun tonight," I said.

"I always have fun," she said.

"Did you like the movie?" I asked.

"I wished I lived in Oz," she said, "instead of here. All they do in Oz is sing."

"Your mole looks really good," I said. "I can't believe how fast you drew it."

"Does it still look good?" she said. "That's nice."

I could tell that all she wanted to do was go home. I should have stopped talking, but I didn't. "Abbey," I said, "I want to tell you something. I really like you. You're a really fun girl to be with."

"Really?" she said.

"Really," I said.

"A really fun girl to be with?" she said.

"That's right," I said.

She lit a cigarette and blew the first puff of smoke straight up like a steam kettle. "God," she exclaimed, "the things young men say when they get horny. Tah-tah, Danny. I'll see you tomorrow night." She left with Zoe and Jay.

I drank a couple more beers with Seth. I felt slightly better, after I had a chance to collect my thoughts.

If romance was like music, which somehow I thought it was, then logic told me it was back to the basics. Back to Mr. Luck.

Yes. I had gotten ahead of myself. Paradiddle. Friggin' paradiddle, paradiddle.

Abbey wanted a drummer. I'd show her a drummer. I knew the drill. First, I would have to make the rudiments sound as they are. Then I would move on....

Chapter 4
The Dameon Inn

Seated several tables away from mine, Abbey was faced so that I saw her striking profile. The lobe of one of her ears, sensuous as an orchid, peaked out from behind streaming brown hair; a silver loop pierced the small wedge of marvelous flesh; on the silver loop hung a single, weightless tropical feather. The dominant smell of Abbey's clove cigarette accented the air in the cocktail lounge, and plumes of white smoke added to her profile's mystique. Zoe sat across from Abbey. Curiously, Abbey was looking past Zoe into empty space. I could hear what they were saying.

"Look at this silver dollar. It was minted in 1936," said Zoe Cleopatra Hash, as she peered down at the top of their cocktail table, scrutinizing old coins which lay submerged under clear varnish, on a bottom of quaint red felt. Abbey's spiritual sister—wearing, as always, a blouse with a sailboat monogrammed on the breast—was hunched over the low table. The tall girl's back curved like a pretty palm tree; her short blonde hair grazed her cheeks.

"I adore history—old places, old dates, old things," Zoe continued. "Do you?"

Abbey remained withdrawn. "Old what?"

"History. Do you think about *time*?"

"I think about San Francisco. I love mints."

"But about time, Abbey?" Zoe persisted. "Isn't it weird to think about a place in time before you were born? About what people did back then?"

Abbey straightened herself and put her elbows on the table.

"Why must you look into plastic tidepools?" she asked.

"The date on that silver dollar struck me. That's all," Zoe said.

"You think too much."

"I do?"

"No, I guess not. It's just that I've never liked history," Abbey told her friend. "Who cares about silver dollars? I'd rather forget everything in the past."

"Oh, I see," Zoe said. "Do you still love him?"

"I love what he gave me. I can't help it...."

Paradiddle. Paradiddle.

I vowed to let my feelings for Abbey lie submerged with Zoe's silver dollar, for a while.

I sipped my gin and tonic. My eyes roamed to a book of matches lying in an ashtray on my table. "The Dameon Inn," the front flap read. The Inn's name looked regal on gloss-white cardboard, each thick, red letter outlined with a filament of gold paint. Everything about this place—attendants and waiters in their red, gold-trimmed suits, old paintings and white linen in the main dining room, bouquets of fresh-cut flowers in the restrooms—seemed to evoke a grand mood. It was the fanciest place in town. It reminded me of my father.

We had come here to play our debut featuring the return of Abbey. A fraternity hired us to play their Spring Formal.

Where I sat in the Stallion Cocktail Lounge, the corner stage was reserved for string quartets and big band jazz. Rock 'n' roll music was banished to the convention room downstairs. A lone man in a tuxedo sat at the piano on the stage, playing a classical-sounding tune—large chords boomed, blended, and rippled on the low keys, while a sharp, cutting melody played over the top in high notes. He seemed full of his song; he played it louder and louder. Conversations quieted, and the older set in the lounge listened appreciatively.

Although the song was rearranged and made to sound

classical, it was still one of *our* songs—a song for youth. The melody was John Lennon's "Imagine." Lennon had recently been gunned down. I wondered, was his song also a tune for the dead?

*   *   *

"Hey, bozo," he said.

"Hey, donkey," I said.

The piano player went back to Beethoven, and Uwe joined me at my table. "This place is outstanding. When my folks come to town, I'm going to put them up here."

"I think it's kind of stuffy."

"You're just a lowly 'band person,'" Uwe mocked. "You're too scummy to appreciate a classy place like this.... Shit, some of my brothers and I ought to take that guy out to pasture and pound his heiny. That bald little maggot."

Uwe was referring to the manager of the Dameon, who had insisted we set up our equipment earlier that afternoon, well in advance of the gig. "It's somewhat inconvenient having you band people dragging your guitars and whatnot in during the dinner hour," he had told Seth, Uwe, and me, when we arrived in the van. The manager herded us with our equipment like we were a bunch of friggin' cattle. He also got all over Uwe for tracking in some mud.

"Hey, girls!" Uwe shouted.

They ignored him.

"What's their problem? Can't they come sit with us? We're in a band together."

"They're talking. Leave them alone."

"Sometimes I think they're lesbos."

"Quiet down a little."

"Okay."

Uwe continued, "I'll tell you something. What they both need is a good hump."

"Jesus."

"I'll pass on Abbey. But I'll bet Zoe is so tight she squeaks. I wouldn't mind giving her the big one."

"You're sick, Uwe."

"Give me a sip of your drink."

"They're $4 a pop. Go thirsty."

"I oughta kick your heiny, Vikker. Later. I'm going to go find Seth and Jay. You and the girlies better come downstairs soon. Let's rock."

"Yeah, later," I said.

* * *

We met in the room the manager assigned to be our dressing area. It was where the Inn's cooks, maids, and groundskeepers changed their uniforms. Against one wall there was a line of solemn, military-gray lockers, labeled with strips of white cloth tape: salt-of-the-earth names written in indelible ink: "Joe," "Harry," "Rita," "Ben," and "Ed"....

Uwe and I didn't need to change for the show. He sat behind keyboards and I sat behind drums; the audience didn't see much of us. Abbey, Seth, and Jay were the front people. They represented the face of Bandit.

Ever since I began playing with them, Seth and Jay had arrived at gigs with suit bags as well as guitars. Jay liked to wear a kimono and knee-high leather boots when he performed. Jay owned three silk kimonos—one royal blue, one pink, and one black.

Seth was not predictable. One night he might wear an old suit and tie purchased from a thrift shop. Another night he would appear looking like an impressionistic billboard, dressed in pants, T-shirt, and tennis shoes covered with all different colors of spray paint. One time Seth painted his entire head light purple, but when Seth got onstage and started to sweat, a couple drops of paint dripped onto his guitar and during break he stripped off the paint with turpentine he had brought in a baby food jar.

Abbey seemed to adore dressing for the show even more than our guitarists. Zoe was helping her get things laid out. The girls hummed with delight.

There was no privacy in our dressing area, but it didn't make her uncomfortable. Quickly, she stripped off her top and pulled on another. Silently, she pulled off jeans and slipped on a short skirt. I felt like a voyeur as I stole a look.

She applied plenty of makeup—black eye liner, red lipstick, and blush. She drizzled tinsel in her hair, and flecks of sparkle on her face.

Her final ensemble for the Dameon gig consisted of a mini-skirt and rose-colored tights; a red, silver, and black sequin-studded blouse; red, rain-slicker boots, and a toy sheriff's badge on her left breast. She looked stunning.

"Here we go," Abbey soon said, as we stood alongside the darkened stage. Beyond us, on the floor, was a vibrant crowd of young men in suits and tuxedos and young women in long, formal gowns.

"Without any further ado," the Sigma Nu's master of ceremonies said into the front and center mike, "I would like to welcome this evening's entertainment—together once again—S.L.O.'s own—Abbey Butler and Bandit."

*   *   *

The first set went great. As Abbey hung on the last word of the set's ending number, I ripped out on my drums. I played triplets trading off between bass drum and tom-toms; I played a vicious series of thirty-second notes on high-toned timbales; I played paradiddles all over the set; I kicked off a couple jazz licks. My solo went on for the sixteen measures predetermined by Seth. On beat four of the second-to-last measure, Seth and Jay jumped into the air and struck final notes when they landed.

Cymbals ringing, Seth and Jay let their fingers crawl up the necks of their guitars, and the pitch lowered and diminished. Abbey took a deep, graceful bow. Seth clicked the foot switch to the stage lights and there was darkness. We slipped off the back of the stage and went to our dressing area.

We broke out a cooler of beer and wine, which was stashed in my bass drum case. Unlike some places, the Dameon didn't offer free drinks to band members. The manager was probably afraid we'd take liberties, maybe converge on the Stallion Cocktail Lounge. Touché. Some of us already had.

We sat on the floor and talked about our music and drank.

Uwe and Abbey got into a mild argument about Bandit choosing a frat party for our debut gig. Abbey said she much preferred playing nightclubs rather than "old-fashioned, dukie proms." I didn't really like playing frats, either, but the fraternities paid four or five times more money than the local nightclubs.

After a while, Seth stood and scrunched up his face at the girls. "Take it easy, you lushes. We have three more sets to go."

Abbey was holding an empty wine bottle.

"I was thirsty," she said, over-emphasizing her words as inebriated people are prone to do.

Zoe laughed.

Seth muttered the word "shit" a number of times. He paced the dressing room. I didn't understand why he was anxious. Abbey always drank a lot.

The Sigma Nu's emcee called us back onstage. It was time for our second set at the Dameon Inn.

Abbey approached her mike. She drew her fingers naughtily through her hair. She grinned devilishly back at the band.

Then she turned and let out a blood-curdling proclamation: "Fuckin' A, all you privileged freaks!"

The crowd was dumb-founded. There was a long, anxious pause.

"Excuse me, I mean Greeks!"

One fraternity guy laughed.

"Are you ready to rock?!" she cried.

A number of people cheered.

She let the audience grow quiet; then, once again, Abbey screamed: "Hey, you rich shits! Does mommy know you're not all virgins?!"

Tension cracked. The audience erupted with laughter and bawdy retorts.

"She's wide open!"

"Crazy bitch!"

"She's totally fresh!"

"Fuckin' A, all you snotty-nosed boys and girls," she dared them. "I guess even bourgeois piggies like to rock 'n' roll!!!"

Her sarcasm was thick enough to cut with a machete, but the voices of her enchanted audience fell in sync with her, "Oink! Oink! Fuckin' A. Dukies like to rock 'n' roll! Oink! Oink! Fuckin' A. Dukies like to rock 'n' roll!"

I had to hand it to her. Somehow, she was managing to stay in control.

Seth grabbed her mike, "This next song is our own version of a Beatles tune, 'Twist and Shout.'"

I kicked in the song hard. Abbey jumped back on track—shut up and started singing. Once again our music sounded awesome with her on vocals.

Song after song went by. Silky dress trains and tuxedo tails whirled on the dance floor.

As we played into the third set, the party became increasingly more rowdy. The frat boys started taking off their ties and their dates started wearing them. During slow numbers, the couples on the dance floor made no attempt to hide their passions. Groin to groin, the carnal grind—guys kneading their girlfriends' bottoms as though they were dough.

Once again, the wine and whatever else she had shared with Zoe surged in her.

"This is no church!" she screamed in between songs. "Goddamnit, I wanna get crazy tonight! I wanna see you dukies tear this place down! I'm the wicked witch. Who are yyyooouuu???"

"Yeah!" the audience whooped. "Party down!!!"

The girl wearing the toy sheriff's badge could do no wrong: she was the law.

The sound of guitars, drums, vocals, and keyboards circled the convention room like a tornado. Jay's bass line thumped in my gut, I pounded on my drums, my arms going limp on the recoils.

Then, nothing came out of the P.A.

Nothing came out of the amps.

The stage lights blinked off.

A bald-headed man stood in the corner by the power supply.

The emcee sauntered over and tried to plug us back in, but the man yanked the cord out of the emcee's hands.

"Bummer," Jay said. "It's him."

The manager made a beeline for the stage.

"It's all well and fine that fraternities have their formals at the Dameon," the bald-headed little man snarled upon reaching us. "We *do* have a policy, however. When the raucousness gets excessive, then 'poof,' we pull the plug on you people."

"'Poof?'" Abbey said, one hip jutted out. "What do you mean 'poof' you pull the plug?"

"Could you please define 'poof?'" Zoe said.

The manager shunted Zoe and focused his glaring eyes on Abbey. "You, miss," he enunciated, "are the crux of the problem. I've been listening to your drivel. You are one of the most vulgar-mouthed female creatures I've ever encountered. Were you raised by cretins?"

Abbey's face blushed.

"That's an awful thing to say, Mr. Whoever-You-Are," Zoe

blurted. "You're worse than a cretin. You're an amoeba."

Abbey still made no reply.

The fraternity boys and their dates began to gather around us.

"I was raised by a goddess," Abbey said finally. Her voice was uneven.

A female voice came from the crowd, "I agree with that man. She does have a slutty mouth. I didn't appreciate some of the things she was saying to us."

"Shut up," a male voice answered. "She's a hot mamma. Talk dirty, baby!"

"Quiet!" the emcee told the crowd. "Look," he said to the manager, "the people at this party didn't do anything wrong. It was the band. We paid money up front for this room. This is one of Sigma Nu's most important functions." He turned on Abbey. "You're a real stupid bitch, aren't you?"

"Don't call me a bitch," Abbey said. "I'm not a bitch."

Seth, the emcee, and the manager removed themselves from the stage to negotiate. I overheard Seth and the emcee trying to convince the manager to let us fire up the P.A. and amps and resume playing. The emcee was persuasive. The manager was stubborn. Seth was frantic.

During all this, Uwe drifted away from the commotion. He stood with a group of prom guests chatting, showing off. He kept putting his arm around this one heavy-set girl; each time he did this, she pushed him away and he laughed.

The rest of the crowd surged toward the bar. Jay, Abbey, Zoe, and I remained on the stage.

"Just look at Uwe," Zoe said.

"God, he's more interested in talking to those dukies than helping Seth get us out of this mess," Abbey said.

"He's so high on himself," Zoe said.

"He's a joke," Abbey said.

"Hey, come on, girls," said Jay, not bothering to look up. He was wiping down his bass. "Give the dude a break. It's all kind of your fault, Abbey. This isn't the first time this has happened, either."

"Shut up, Jay."

I said nothing. I felt bad for her, but I couldn't think of how to defend her.

I noticed Uwe go over and join in with Seth, the manager, and the emcee. The manager had stopped shouting.

They called the rest of us over.

"We've got two choices," Seth explained. "One is we pack up and leave and don't get paid."

"The other choice is this," Uwe cut in. "The manager and my colleagues in Sigma Nu feel the guests of this party and the rest of the members of Bandit should not be penalized just because the lead singer has a trashy mouth." He straightened his back and looked down at Abbey. "I told these people about your problem, Abbey—about how you were kicked out of school for the same reason, being a slut."

"Shut up," said Abbey.

"Can it, Uwe," said Jay. "You're being way too harsh."

"This is ridiculous," said the manager.

"Sir, let me talk," Uwe said. "Everyone in the band, except Vikker, knows it was her who Domino got sick of. This time she needs to leave. We finish the gig without her, and without anymore of her trash."

The manager said, "She is not the type of person we want presiding over a function at the Dameon." Both the manager and Uwe acted as if Abbey were invisible.

"Let's bail," said Jay.

"This is bogus," I said.

"What will it be, people?" the manager asked.

Seth put a hand on Abbey's shoulder. "It's not like we're kicking you out. We'll just finish the gig with the stuff Jay and I sing."

The emcee said, "You said you'd tell her to leave." He, too, refused to look at Abbey directly. She was crying. Zoe was crying, too.

"Yeah, tell her to get her butt out of here," some frat guy yelled.

I looked around for him. I wanted to sock him. But it was a zoo. I couldn't single out one smart-ass dukie from another.

My eyes returned to where Abbey and Zoe had been standing.

Zoe remained. Abbey was gone.

Zoe delivered a message from Abbey: "She wants you to keep playing tonight without her, and if you don't she's gonna quit the band. You know she'll do it, too." She looked coldly at Uwe. "This isn't going to happen again."

"Is that a threat?" said Uwe.

Zoe stormed off. A drunken frat guy bellowed, "Watch out. She's a hot mamma, too."

Seth rallied us together. He told us we better play spectacularly if we wanted to get paid. I didn't say anything, neither did Jay.

I felt ashamed for Abbey. I also felt paranoid that there was a chance I might not ever see her again.

Chapter 5
Suspenders

What exactly is it about men who wear suspenders? Do they belong to a cult? Do they idolize firemen or lumberjacks? Is it that they have a strange phobia toward belts—are belts a gripping fear around their waists? Did their fathers strap them, and do suspenders symbolize emancipation? Suspenders, it would seem, are of little use except to hold one's pants up, and Uwe's jeans screamed at his hefty waistline and clung to his thick, Nordic legs like Scotch tape. Two wide, rainbow-colored suspenders decorated his shoulders, each strap tensionless as a slice of headcheese. Uwe looked absurd.

I drummed absently on my thighs as I gazed through the Coffee Shack's tinted windows. The theme song from the television sitcom Barney Miller had been playing in the back of my mind all day long since my eight o'clock Non-Euclidean Geometry class. Uwe was outside in the campus courtyard with a bunch of his fraternity brothers. It was too bright outside for him to look in and see us. The differential intensity of the afternoon sunshine and the dark-oak dimness inside the Coffee Shack made the cafe's tinted windows into one-way mirrors.

If Uwe hadn't been outside, Zoe probably would have finished her Coca-Cola and left. She wasn't one to idle away her time in the campus snackbar as I sometimes did. The vicarious intrigue of spying on Uwe was altogether too compelling, however, and kept Zoe from going off to class or to the library.

All of the other Alpha Upsilons were wearing showy rainbow suspenders like Uwe. "It must be some kind of brotherhood-love thing to wear those," she said.

"Must be."

"Dukies are such peacocks, aren't they?"

"I'm sure Abbey would liken them to something much worse."

"Oh my."

Bandit had played several gigs since the Sigma Nu incident, and Abbey had toned down her stage act considerably. She apologized to all of us, including Uwe. We all agreed that the matter should be dropped.

However, in a cleverly vague way, Uwe continued to gloat over his triumph. And in an overtly blatant way, Abbey continued to despise him.

Yet a strong force held Abbey, Uwe, Seth, and Jay together —something about the band's past with Domino. I was sucked into a vacuum the ex-drummer left.

"I wonder what Uwe and company are plotting," I said. "Another controversial hazing up at the Ag barns?"

"Perhaps," said Zoe, "a multiple sheep rape."

"Let's see if we can read their lips."

"Oh my, that one fellow just said he wants to bring a blindfold."

"Of course Uwe's in charge of the gumboots."

"I really can't stand him." She sighed.

"We're stuck with him."

"Yes."

"It has something to do with Domino, doesn't it?"

This was the first time I'd mentioned his name in the presence of one of the girls.

Zoe pretended like she didn't hear me.

She made a funny face at Uwe through our one-way mirror, and sipped the rest of her coke through a straw until there was just ice and a gurgling noise.

After a while she said, "East is east. West is west. Zoe-baby is the best."

"What?"

"Isn't that warped?"

"Yes, what are you talking about?"

"Uwe," she said. "The other night at practice, he stole my biochemistry text. He was acting like a jerk, as usual. The next day I discovered a bunch of notes in it."

"What did they say?"

"Stuff. The east-west-best business was the most bizarre. He wrote it on page 217, at the beginning of the chapter on cellular reproduction. He also drew a man's penis."

I felt like going outside and wrapping Uwe's suspenders around his neck. He had no right to bug Zoe. She was too friggin' nice.

"Did you say something to him?"

"What could I say?"

"Maybe you should have confronted him," I said. "Or maybe I should—maybe Jay or Seth?"

"My hero!" she teased. "Don't worry, Danny, Abbey will always hate him enough for both of us. She's working on Seth and Jay."

"What do you mean?"

"Just drop it."

Outside, Uwe and his buddies began to split. One of them snapped Uwe's suspenders against his back. He spun around to look for the guy who did it. He couldn't find him; so he stood wearing a frown. He reached down and picked at the seat of his underwear before walking away. The sonofabitch didn't know anyone was watching.

"Oh my," I said, imitating Zoe's favorite expression.

"I better go," she said.

"Have another coke," I said. "Why the hurry?"

"I have to keep my grades up," she said. "Someday I might want to go to law school or something."

Yeah, I thought, and someday soon I would *not* want to go

to Stanford Graduate School, but I would go there anyway.

Zoe picked up her book bag and started to leave. Then, rather tentatively, she hung back. "Abbey and I are going to Santa Barbara to visit Abbey's mother on Saturday. Seth was going to lend us his V.W., but it isn't working."

"I see."

"This presents a problem."

"I could drive you two."

"That's what I hoped you'd say."

What a coup, I thought.

"Look for me on Saturday, then," I said. "I'll be wearing suspenders."

"Don't you dare," she said.

*   *   *

That night I went to 29 Orchid Street for a midweek practice. We were introducing a couple more of Seth's originals into our show. Seth refused to play new pieces at a gig until we polished them to death. By the end of practice we were all a bit put out by his obsessiveness.

This also was the night he asked us to pledge our futures to Bandit.

We were presently a hometown band, playing to a loyal hometown audience. To Seth, true success as a nightclub band meant playing new towns and bigger clubs; it meant being good enough to break new ice night after night. Seth claimed we would never know how good Bandit was until we got out of S.L.O.

He had brought all this up before. But except for Jay, who was game for anything, all of us, Abbey included, had been noncommittal. Uwe had had two interviews with a company in L.A. and had a job offer after graduation. Abbey was closely moored to her mother in Santa Barbara; she was reluctant to move farther away. I had plans, too.

But Seth now had something working in his favor. A song by the Pricey Dexters, featuring none other than Domino Gettsland on drums, had broken onto the charts. Suddenly, Bandit's ex-drummer had become famous, and Bandit's remaining, die-hard members were green with envy. Domino's big splash made me feel restless, too. Something competitive boiled inside me—I needed to try and match this guy, beat for beat. "Where do you think we should go?" I asked Seth.

"I don't think we're ready to go south to L.A." he replied. "We need more experience. We don't have enough originals." His fingers nervously ghosted chords on the neck of his guitar. "But I've talked to some other people in bands like ours who've headed to northern California. This one cat in S.B. told me about Lake Tahoe. There's a new music scene taking root there. It's the type of place where a band like us can transition—from small-time to professional."

"It's perfect," Abbey said. "Bandit's a rebel band, and playing L.A. right now would be a cliché. I'm sure northern California has great clubs."

"We'll blow Tahoe away," said Jay.

"I just don't get it," Uwe said. "The industry is south. What a bunch of donkeys! You guys are scared of Domino, aren't you?"

"This sounds cool, Uwe. Come on," said Jay. "If things gel, we'll get down south."

"The Sierras are beautiful," Zoe said dreamily, as she browsed through one of her notebooks. "I'd love to summer there."

"You can be our manager," exclaimed Abbey.

"Yes, I could," Zoe said.

"She's dead wood," Uwe said. "Seth does fine managing us. If you go, Zoe, you're going to have to earn your own way." He puckered his liver lips and blew her a kiss.

"You goon," said Abbey.

Seth looked at Abbey and Zoe and rolled his eyes. "Trust

me," he said to Uwe. "This is the right move for us."

"Consider it, Uwe," said Jay. "Do you really to want to wear a suit and tie and kiss the Man's heiny every day? L.A.'s tough, dude—competitive and expensive. You'll just end up 9-to-5-ing for that company that's got its eye on you. Hey, man, we gotta let this band ripen on the vine." Jay grinned. He liked his last line.

"So it's all set in cement?" Uwe asked.

Everyone nodded.

Uwe rose and thrust out his big right hand. "Put your hands on mine. We do this in my frat for spirit."

Abbey smirked and thrust out her hand limp-wristed.

"You too, Zoe," he said.

Our voices echoed his. "Alpha, two, Upsilon, four. Go, Bandit, pound the floor!"

I looked around me. Everyone seemed embarrassed, yet also very, very happy. We're a strange bunch, I thought—however, right then, I liked everyone, almost loved everyone, even Uwe.

Uwe started laughing. The rest of us laughed, too, but Uwe kept it up—eyes watering, growing hysterical.

"What's his problem?" Abbey said.

"He's just totally stoked—aren't you, Uwe?" Jay said.

"No, you stupid chink. That's not it."

Uwe dried his eyes with Jay's bass wipe. "This whole thing—to watch it play out—it's fuckin' hilarious."

"Huh?"

"When push came to shove, I knew you guys didn't have the guts to head south, to really go for it. It's just like he said it would be."

"What are you talking about?" Abbey demanded.

"Domino gave me a call the other night," Uwe said. "He wanted to check in with his old pal, you know. Of course he rubbed his hit song in my face, you know how he is.

"We talked about my getting a job in L.A. I said I wanted to get in another band, something with promise. Domino said

L.A. is full of opportunities for keyboard players like me. He practically dared me to quit you guys and come hang out with him. He's going to crack up when I tell him about your 'big plans' in Tahoe. You bunch of losers!"

Uwe turned his eyes on Abbey. "He also asked about you, Abbey. I told him you were still fucking up—still a drunken, stoned, head case."

"Asshole!" Abbey rushed at him and hit him in the stomach.

"Get her off me, guys," Uwe barked, "or I'll hit her back."

Jay grabbed Abbey. I was frozen. Seth stood up and started toward Uwe.

"You want some, too, little donkey?" Uwe's eyes burned.

"You're out, man. That's it," Seth said.

"Don't think about coming back," said Abbey.

"Outstanding," Uwe said smugly. "Now excuse me, I've got a future to embark upon, and you losers aren't in it."

Jay grudgingly helped Uwe clear his stuff out of the studio and load it in his car. The rest of us went inside the house. We could hear them shouting at each other while they were working. Then we heard Uwe's car roar away, the horn blaring the length of Orchid Street.

Jay came inside and asked for the bong. He sat down and took a giant hit. He leaned forward and rested his elbows on his knees and covered his face with his hands. He was silent for a long time; then he looked up.

"I have something to confess," he said. "I've given Domino a few calls myself—you know, we've always been buds, and then I had to congratulate him."

"Another traitor," Abbey said.

"It wasn't like I was kissing his ass. It was hard, Abbey. I have my pride.

"Anyway, we rapped about his thing down there. He asked how Bandit was doing and I told him we were doing okay, that we might start gigging outside of S.L.O. He was cool. He even gave me some advice."

"You're going down there, too?" I said.

"That's shit," said Seth.

"No, he didn't invite me. What he said is that we ought to get rid of Uwe, that he was dead weight.

"I said that was kind of harsh, and then he said not really, that Uwe has called *him* a bunch of times, not vice versa. Uwe's, like, hounding Domino to get him into the music scene in L.A. Uwe's the donkey. He's only out for himself."

"That asshole," Seth said. "Domino's right, we don't need Uwe. We'll do better without him. So what if he was an original member."

"I'm glad you feel that way," Jay said, "because here's the deal—I sort of asked Domino to lead Uwe on a little, you know, get on the phone and act like he's glad to hear from Uwe, let him think there *are* opportunities for him in L.A. Give the dude some bait, you know, then blow him off when he gets down there."

"Wicked," I said.

"Domino said he'd do it?" Abbey asked.

"He did it. It's done."

Jay looked at Seth. "I feel guilty, dude."

"I wish you would've talked to me first," Seth said. "But, shit, I guess I've reached my limit with that donkey." He issued a polka-dotted party horn laugh.

"Finally," Zoe said.

"You're brilliant," Abbey said. She rushed over and gave Jay a hug. So did Zoe. I was happy for him, but I wished the girls were hugging me.

*   *   *

The point where Highway 101 breaks out of the rolling coastal hills and jags south in order to parallel the ocean was my favorite part of the drive to Santa Barbara. Gaviota blinked by and then there was a concert of water—blue, alive, and shimmering. This wide-angle picture slugged a person wide awake and sent tingles through the stomach to the groin.

That Saturday morning, crisp, cool air found its way into the passenger cab of my truck through the cracked wing windows while a contrast of eastward sun baked my lap; the fresh air and sun titillated my body hot/cold, hot/cold—yielding a soothing average warmness.

"Isn't the ocean beautiful," Abbey said. "It makes me high." She sat in the middle of my Toyota pickup's small cab. Gazing at the sparkling Pacific, she leaned against me and stayed there for a long while. Her body conducted a smooth, elegant warmth—snug as an electric blanket.

My dreamy thoughts bobbed like pieces of cork. I imagined Seth, Jay, Abbey, and myself to be shells on the beach. Different shells, each with a different color, shape, and spindly sharpness. Seth was an old shell—bone-white, weathered, and wise. Jay was an oval shell, pearl-pink on the inside, with a fan of unicorn horns splayed outward around the opening. Abbey was an oyster-sized abalone, the walls inside and out a blue-swirl jewel. I was not a shell, really, but a smooth piece of quartz the size of a very small potato. In my shell metamorphosis, the sand on my belly felt like wet gravel.

Zoe was there, too, crawling around the clean sand where the shells lay. She was a young female sand crab. I wasn't sure, exactly, what the difference was between a male and female sand crab, but I knew this to be a girl-crab. Her shell had a metallic sheen and was the same light, red-orange color as a newborn human.

Uwe appeared. He was a man in suspenders smoking a cigar. He walked along the surf line with a mutt dog. Uwe stood to one side of the circle of shells, the rock, and the sand crab, while his dog grimaced and lowered its haunches and took a giant crap in foamy inch-deep water.

The image snapped off.

Abbey asked why I flinched. I told her it was too weird to talk about.

The song on the radio ended with a rim shot, and the D.J. said, "Hey out there! Here we go with that new hip sensation, the Pricey Dexters. The tune's called 'Runnin' like Cecelia.' And the big P.D. is runnin' hot...."

"Big P.D.? Oh my, now they even have their own acronym," Zoe said. "And it's almost phallic." Her nose was in a notebook, and she was talking more to herself than to Abbey or me.

"Over and over and OVER," Abbey said, "the radio stations play this stupid song. I'm so tired of hearing Domino and *that band*. Can we put in a cassette tape?"

I started to load *The Pretenders* with Chrissie Hynde, one of Abbey's favorites, into the deck.

"No," Abbey told me. "Wait. I'm going to handle this thing like a professional. There, I'm listening. I'm trying to learn something musically.... Shit...."

"Runnin' like Cecelia" was, I hated to admit, a catchy tune—a real rocker. And I had no doubt that the song's big beat contributed to its chartbusting success. In a few places, I couldn't follow his drum work. Some of the beats and fills were so slick they eluded me. Damn he was good. Every time I heard "Runnin' like Cecelia," I was reminded of Domino's skillful drumming. And the D.J.s kept playing the song over and over and *over*.

> *Sin city's just plastic baby*
> *Red lovin', bets on checkers maybe*
> *You strut on heels and tear down lives*
> *Witchy girl burn fire, fire*
>
> *Runnin' like Cecelia*
> *Runnin' like Cecelia....*

Like most rock 'n' roll songs, the lyrics were simple, but the way the singer sang them caused the words to strike a nerve. The P.D.'s lead singer strove to affect the visceral rather than the aesthetic. Lyrics, melody, and rhythm of "Runnin' like Cecelia" all were raw and good.

I hated Domino. I admired Domino. Then I hated him some more.

The waves opposite the highway looked small and shapely, churning over beds of kelp. As we drove along, I pointed out a few surfers, but neither girl displayed much interest. Abbey began to file her nails with quick, nervous strokes. Scratch, scratch, scratch—a rushed, annoying rhythm. Zoe's glasses had slipped to the end of her nose. She stared into a macroeconomics text propped in her lap. One of Zoe's hands gripped the book; Zoe's other hand, moving as rapidly as Abbey's nail file, located and traced important lines of text, highlighting them in fluorescent yellow for later review.

"I think I'll paint every other nail white and every other one bright red," Abbey announced. She held out both hands and examined them, then went back to filing.

During her manicure and Zoe's studying, I began to think about Santa Barbara. I had heard bits and pieces about Isabella from Jay. Jay said he met her once when she was in S.L.O. visiting Abbey. Abbey asked Jay to drive her mother, Zoe, and her to the beach in the van and Isabella took the four of them out to lunch at the Custom House in Avila. Her generosity impressed Jay, who always welcomed a free meal.

"Abbey acts like she's on Cloud 9 when her mom's around. Her mother is cool. It's no fake, dude. Abbey really digs her."

Mrs. Butler owned a leather goods shop in Santa Barbara. Abbey and Zoe had earrings and purses from there. Twice a month, like clockwork, Abbey and Zoe would trek to Santa Barbara to visit Isabella. They usually borrowed Seth's V.W. and went alone.

Today's proposed agenda proved to be a little disappointing. Abbey made it clear that she wanted to spend some time alone with her mother, so Zoe suggested the two of us go to the beach. There was also a music store that I wanted to visit. We had a gig that night at Chee's Nightclub, and Seth, of course, was expecting us to be there, or else. I hoped Abbey would fit me into her busy schedule. But I wasn't counting on anything. What was new?

When we reached the outskirts of the city, Zoe shut her textbook and put it into her handbag full of magic markers, notes, and miscellaneous feminine apparel. Acting very pleased with herself as she always did when she accomplished a long stretch of studying, she blurted, "Oh, Abbey, I can't wait to see Izy."

Abbey located her purse under the bench seat and began to brush her long brown hair with deliberate strokes. "Turn off at the next exit," she told me. "My mother lives down by the water. Her shop's close by."

I decelerated to 25 mph and rolled down my window. It was noontime, the sun was strong, and there wasn't a cloud in the sky. Sea spice saturated the air.

We were in an older section of town. The streets were narrow and the storefronts high and canopied. A curious assortment of people strolled on the sidewalks. Some of them were locals wearing sandals, shorts, and loose-fitting tops; some of them were tourists wearing the same getup. It was easy to distinguish between the locals and the tourists. The locals' skin was bronze and their hair stained yellow from salt and sun; the tourists' skin was either milky white or painfully red.

"Here it is," Abbey said.

"Isabella's Leather Shoppe," the sign read. It was a tiny shop squeezed between a bookstore and a place that sold Swedish furniture. Blue paint, white trim, and quaint white wooden shutters gave the shop a cheery face. The front door stood open, held that way by a hefty potted plant.

Seven or eight customers browsed inside. One old man picked up a leather handbag and smelled it. His wife was nearby, in front of a display of sand-casted candles. "What are you doing?" she asked.

A woman parted a cloth drape and emerged from the rear of the store carrying a box filled with cards and envelopes. "Oh there you girls are," the woman said, her voice throaty and musical like Abbey's. "I was just putting these new greeting cards out. Carmen did a lovely job on them. His new poems are *very* sensitive." Her eyes traveled past Abbey and Zoe to me. "You must be Danny, the drummer," she said. "I'm Abbey's mother, Isabella. The girls call me Izy."

Isabella's hair was tinged gray and left long and flowing, not done up in a beauty parlor hairdo like my mother's. Her skin creased around her eyes and showed age; but still, it was taut and elegant, especially around her sharp cheekbones. Izy was taller than her daughter, and she had a more springy walk. She was strikingly pretty, like a china teacup.

"Hello," I said.

I learned that the author of the verse on the greeting cards was a local poet and friend of Isabella's. Zoe whispered that Carmen and Izy were lovers. The girls helped Izy put the cards on display while I looked at the many purses, belts, and wallets distributed around the shop on hooks and in wooden bins. The shop's interior smelled richly of leather, and I, too, felt a strange need to pick up articles of tanned hide and rub them against my face and inhale their musky scent.

"I'll shoo the customers out of here shortly and close up," Izy said. "Now Zoe, dear, and Danny, you two will pick up Abbey later?"

"That's the plan," I said.

"Good, then we all can have a nice visit," Izy said.

*   *   *

Zoe and I had lunch at a little outdoor restaurant. It was good in a way that Abbey hadn't joined us because she never ate regular meals and always got bored at restaurants. Abbey was a nibbler and relied on frozen yogurt and nachos to keep herself nourished. Fortunately, Zoe had a hearty appetite like mine.

We finished our coffee and walked to a music shop Seth had recommended. Seth claimed Granger's Music was the only decent place to buy anything musical north of L.A.

Inside, Granger's looked like a warehouse. There were rows and rows of drum kits stacked bass drum on the bottom with successively smaller drums stacked on top, forming perfect pyramids of concentricity. There were walls and walls of guitars, amps, and keyboards as well.

I didn't need a new drum set. My blue swirl seven-piece Sonor was a real prize, and I had no plans to trade it in. What I wanted was another cymbal—a twelve-inch thin crash Zildjian. Twelve inchers had a far-out, spanky sound. I located precisely what I wanted. Unfortunately it cost twice as much as I could afford—that was without a stand. I was low on cash. I made a little money playing with Bandit, but I hadn't received any checks from home for a while. And I wasn't expecting any.

"Can I help you find something?" said a salesperson. He was missing the lower part of his left arm and had a fake hand, the kind with cables and a stainless steel pincher.

"These cymbals ever go on sale?" I asked, my eyes dropping to his artificial hand as if it were a nudey photo. I felt like a creep.

"They're already marked down," he replied. "But I like to deal. Which ones are you interested in?"

I tried to stare at his eyes instead. "I think I'm just looking," I said.

"How long have you played drums?" he asked.

"Ever since I was a kid," I said.

"Same here," he said. "Until the auto wreck." He clipped his pincher together to demonstrate how it worked. "I've got no wrist-action in this hand. So I can't drum. Never mind, I thank Lord Jesus for my life all the same."

Good God, I felt like a lucky slob. "I'm sorry," I said.

"Thanks, brother," he said. "Let me know if you need any assistance, okay?"

The salesman moved toward a young boy and his mother. The young boy was fondling everything in sight, including the cymbals on a drum kit display. There's nothing worse for the finish of virgin brass than corrosive, oily finger prints. There's nothing more irritating to a drummer or to a salesman.

"Please don't touch the cymbals."

"Nope. I don't wanna."

The salesman steered the little boy away from the drum set with his one good arm.

"Jason, you get away from that man this instant," the boy's mother said.

The kid didn't mind his mother, either. He banged on a crash cymbal with his fat little fist.

Being a drummer, I couldn't help myself. The Good Salesman was being too nice for his own good. "Hey lady, do everyone a favor and get your brat away from those," I said. "Do you realize how much those things cost? They're no good if they have finger prints all over them."

"That's correct," the salesman said.

"Well, I never!" the woman said. She left dragging the little shit by his elastic suspenders, and right before she walked out the front entrance she stopped and slapped the little boy hard on the rear.

The salesman looked up toward the ceiling with an apologetic face. "Forgive me, Lord."

"Little boys wearing suspenders bug me," I said.

"Bless him. May Lord Jesus give him strength," the salesman said. He turned to me. "May the Lord also give you strength, my friend, and me, as well."

"What?" I said.

"I don't like suspenders either," he said with a gracious laugh; then he looked upward.

I left the Good Salesman to pray.

I found Zoe looking at a Moog synthesizer. I asked her if she played.

"No," she replied, "I don't play any instrument at all. In my family, cultivating music is more important than playing it. Ironic, huh?"

"No instrument at all? Not even a clarinet or something like that when you were younger, in junior high or high school?"

"Not even a bassoon," she said. She held an imaginary bassoon in her hands and danced. Because she was tall, Zoe wasn't the most coordinated person in the world. Her dancing was so innocent and cute that I wanted to give her a hug. I didn't, however.

"Isn't this one lovely?" she said, pointing to a baby grand piano with a jet-black finish. "My parents have one just like it. No one plays it, of course. It's just for looks."

We sat on the bench and Zoe began to play full chords. I listened to the sound resonate on the strings and in the piano's dense, fragrant wood.

"I thought you didn't play," I said.

"Just enough to fool people," she said. "I know a little Chopin, and a few recital classics like 'Chopsticks' and the 'Baby Elephant Walk.'"

I laughed.

"I wish I could play and sing like Abbey. That would be wonderful." Her voice seemed a little envious.

"Do you know who taught Abbey to play?" she continued. "It was Isabella. She has a Ph.D. in Music Theory. Isn't that impressive?"

"Why doesn't she teach music instead of running that shop?" I asked.

"She taught Abbey rather well, don't you think?"

"Yes, she did. It's just curious."

"Yes it is," Zoe admitted. "One time Izy told me that she was the way she is because all she ever wanted to be was an artist, nothing else. I'm not sure what she meant exactly."

*   *   *

It was nearly four o'clock when Zoe and I went to Izy's apartment. The band was supposed to meet at Chee's Nightclub in Pismo Beach at seven; so we couldn't stay at Izy's for long. We had over an hour of driving ahead of us, and when we got to Chee's we needed to change and set up.

Isabella's apartment was on the beach four or five blocks from her shop. All of the apartment entrances faced the ocean, and the view was especially good from the second level, where Izy's place was. A hand-painted sign hung in one corner of the the terraced entry. The sign read: "This Lovely Sea Nest of Mine."

As Zoe knocked, I looked back at the sea, the same sea that parallels Highway 101 from Gaviota to Ventura—a strip of ocean I've always thought to be special because of the way it glistens. Even the oil rigs dotting the horizon did not take away from the shimmering blueness of this stretch of the Pacific.

Abbey answered the door and said brightly, "Hi, you two. Have fun?"

"Hello, kids," Isabella called from somewhere inside. It felt pleasant, in a way, to be referred to as a kid.

"Zoe and I almost bought a bassoon," I said to Abbey. I was glad to see her.

"That's very nice, Danny," she said. She winked at Zoe. "Sit down. Isabella and I made cookies."

The inside of Isabella's apartment smelled like spice and cinnamon. I admired her collection of paintings—local scenes of the Central California coast. In one corner of the front room, there was a baby grand piano like the one Zoe had been drawn to at Granger's, only this piano was older. The baby grand took half of the floor space in the small room. A well-used violin sat upright in a straw basket next to the piano. Also, curiously, there was a shelf opposite the piano lined with stuffed animals and toys. In the kitchen, I could see there was a highchair.

"Nice place," I said to Abbey.

"You should compliment Izy, not me."

"Those aren't your old toys, are they?" I teased, pointing to the shelf. "It's hard to imagine Bandit's rock 'n' roll queen playing with that junk."

Abbey's voice took a sharp edge. "His play things are not junk! What a crude thing to say."

"Carmen has a young child," Zoe interjected. "And Izy baby-sits. Those are his toys, not Abbey's."

"His name is Hector and he's an angel," Abbey said.

I said I was sorry. "I'm sorry, okay?" I repeated.

Abbey and Zoe exchanged one of their secret looks, and Abbey cooled off. She went to help her mother in the kitchen, and as she passed, she patted me on the head. Good God, I thought, one minute she's as volatile as friggin' nitroglycerin, the next minute she treats me as if I were her pet. Vikker, I mused, you picked one hell of a girl to be ga-ga over.

Izy brought a tray of cinnamon snaps and offered us tea. Abbey told her mother she would prefer white wine. When Isabella returned with the drinks, Zoe pulled a joint out of her purse and sparked it.

"Good thought," Abbey said.

Isabella reappeared and said in an exhaustive tone, "Fiddlesticks. You girls and your habits." She turned to me. "Don't let them corrupt you, Danny." Zoe handed the joint to Abbey, and Abbey handed it to her mother, who took a long, expert drag.

The four of us started talking—talking and talking—about

nothing in particular—the usual profound garbage that people chat about when they're high: "these cookies taste sooo delicious...that blouse is sooo purple...his verse is sooo sublime...everything is cool...."

Then I drifted away from the conversation. My thoughts became crystal clear.

All I ever wanted to be was a drummer....

Had this always been the truth? Had drums, music, partying—all the things my father labeled "crap" (and Jay Wong labeled "bitchin'")—had these things propelled me to become who I really was, or had they changed me into something different?

Thinking about this frightened me—because until I resolved this question, the nitpicky analytical side of me wouldn't allow me to factor out the sobering possibility that I'd turned into a weed-smoking, coke-snorting, heavy-drinking, "C"-grade loser.

Yet a bigger part of me knew that I was a good drummer, and that I currently liked myself better than I ever had before. Being a doctor's son had never been fun.

I had always hated his idea of what I should be, because I could never seem to do it well enough to merit his endorsement and pride.

I loved playing drums with Bandit. That was a given. And, of course, I loved Abbey.

I felt kinship toward all the members of Bandit like I'd never felt for family and friends. I'd only known Abbey's mother for about four hours yet I felt more comfortable around her than my own parents. And there was a part of me that pained to acknowledge this. I supposed I could contact the graduate schools, mend fences, get back on track....

I knew going to Tahoe would make things worse. But, fuck it. I was going—that was all there was to it. From that point on, I resolved to not look back!

Chapter 6
Lake Tahoe, California–Nevada

Sometimes a fool gets lucky and wins
Sometimes an old man dies for a young man's sins
But when the amber light
Of day is gone
All I want to feel
Is the beat of a heart....
   — Patty Smyth and Scandal

I know
It's only rock 'n' roll
But I like it, like it
Yes I do....
   — The Rolling Stones

Summer 1981

"Freedom!" Jay yelled, as he leapt off the end of the pier. For a moment he seemed to hover—neither rising nor falling, suspended like a cartoon hero; then gravity yanked him, and he flopped into the icy blue water. Within seconds Jay reappeared, lunging upward and exposing nearly all of his torso. "You bullshitted me, Vikker," he screamed. "This water's colder than ice."

"You donkey," I said from the pier. "What do you expect? This is Tahoe. It ain't Hawaii, partner. We're at 6,000 feet." I dove in, too.

I hadn't swum in Lake Tahoe for a long time, since four or five years back when my family vacationed in a Sierra condo. The clean, clear, dark blue water engulfed me, and its coldness quickly penetrated my arms and legs and chest. At first the lake water caused me to gasp, but soon I was numb to the cold, full of exuberance. It was ten or twelve feet deep off the end of Schooner Pier. Jay and I were treading water and wrestling around like teenagers.

"Come on in, Seth," I said to our guitarist, who was standing next to Abbey and Zoe on the wooden pier. Abbey sat royally in a beach chair and smoked a cigarette. Zoe was stretched out in the afternoon sun, wearing baggy Bermuda shorts and a flower-print micro-bikini top. Zoe, our newly self-appointed manager, was becoming a bit more risqué.

Seth nervously paced the edge of the pier, trying to gather enough courage to jump in after Jay and me.

"I don't swim so good," he repeated.

Jay blew a mouthful of water into the air like a whale, then instructed Seth to paddle out on the surfboard. I watched a discreet smile form on Jay's lips. "As soon as he's out here," Jay whispered, "one of us should tip him."

"What's so funny," Seth yelled. "What the fuck is so funny?" Awkwardly, he lowered the surfboard into the water and climbed onto it. The squirrelly competition surfboard teetered from side to side as he paddled out.

I dove underwater and felt a gradient of cold as I got deeper. The water was chilly on my eyes, and in the fishbowl blur, I made out a white sandy bottom and a few pieces of water-logged driftwood; around me was a matrix of turquoise blue; above me, I saw Jay's legs and the long, oval belly of the surfboard. I planted my feet in the sand, remembering my need for oxygen, and torpedoed into Seth.

Seth was right when he said he couldn't swim well. He lost hold of the surfboard and floundered and dog-paddled back to the pier swearing, "Danny, you fucker. You fucker." Jay did a smooth, showy backcrawl and escorted Seth in.

I hung on the surfboard about 75 feet out and floated.

It was quieter without Jay and Seth in the lake. I listened to water flapping lazily against the surfboard. Damn, I thought. Here we are—in Tahoe.

We didn't have a place to stay, any jobs, and only enough money to last for two or three weeks. We were car camping in my pickup and the van. What we needed was a couple rooms—with showers and toilets and beds—somewhere to spread out, to set up our instruments, to hone our act.

Nevertheless, the situation felt good—really friggin' good—much more peaceful, much more harmonious, than things had been just before we left San Luis Obispo.

We had hoped to get some cash together for our tour by playing a number of end-of-the-year frat parties, but four out of five of those jobs fell through. With all the anti-Bandit sentiment that Uwe stirred up among the Greeks, it was a wonder we retained the one job with the Tau Deltas. It was a bush gig. The crowd acted blasé toward us and our music, and this gravely offended Abbey. But no matter what she screamed into her mike, she mustered no power over them—the dukies refused to act like dukies.

We did go out with a bang at Chee's Nightclub and at Aces. Each place had a special going away theme for our last shows. Aces called our final gig "Bandit's '81 Tour Kick-off" and served double kamikazes for 59 cents a pop. Chee's did a similar thing, not to be one-upped, and called our last night there "Bandit's Dead Brain Cell Festival."

At both gigs everyone in the place got totally ripped, including the band; although, despite all the booze, we played pretty well.

Spook's going away party was, by far, the best.

He and some other groupies threw an outrageous bash at

his place. The highlight was a strange, dramatic presentation of a monument to Bandit, which Spook had designed himself.

He waited till midnight, then swept away the object's huge, red-silk veil. There, underneath, was a baked serpent, constructed out of countless rectangular sections of chocolate cake, all laid out decorously on a row of card tables covered with wax paper.

An aluminum foil horn protruded from the creature's head. Wings made from coat hangers and plastic garbage sacks stretched out from the middle of its body. Fishing line anchored the wing tips to the ceiling. Spook had even hooked up rubber hoses to a bowl of dry ice, so that smoke spewed from the serpent's nostrils. And it must have taken him days to tile the entire creature with the brown and green M&Ms that served as scales.

Spook allowed everyone time for a reverent viewing of the creature; then he ceremoniously hacked off the serpent's head with an army surplus machete. The guests ate pieces of serpent with glasses of keg beer.

During the festivities Abbey and Zoe became very drunk and lively. I asked Abbey to dance six times. She said yes only once.

Right-left-right-right. Left-right-left-left. My thoughts could not linger on the rudiments of love.

I had my glorious diploma, and had received letters of acceptance from several graduate schools. I thanked the graduate schools genuinely for their offers, and asked them all for a rain check.

After commencement ceremonies, I explained my plan to drum now and defer graduate mathematics till later. His reply: "Crap. Goddamn crap! You're a selfish person, Danny. I break my back for you. I send you to school. I give you love and everything you want. And all I asked for in return is to have a respectable, educated son. Now you want to cash in everything and become a loser?"

"That's not it at all, Dad," I said.

"Shut up," he said. "Shut up and listen to me." His hand latched onto the back of my neck. I thought he was going to shake me, like he did when I was a little kid.

He lifted up my collar and said, "Good Lord." I realized he was commenting on my clip-on necktie. For him there was no substitute for the convention of a real necktie and a smartly tied double Windsor knot.

"Look at you," he said. "These people in this group, or combo, or whatever you call yourselves obviously are derelicts. What the hell is wrong with you? Is it pot, cocaine? Tell me! I'm a doctor, or have you forgotten?"

"Dad, don't you understand? I've never felt better."

"Shut up," he said. "When you straighten up, let me know. Until then, you're on your own, buster."

"Aren't I already?" I asked.

He pulled a fifty dollar bill from his wallet. "I was going to give you $5,000 for graduation. I thought you might want a new car, or a trip to Hawaii, or something special. But you don't deserve it. So I'm knocking off two zeros." He paused and his expression thawed a little. "If you change your mind about grad school, ha-ha, you're back to four figs. What do you think about that, math wiz?"

It took me a moment to gather some courage. "$50 minus $50 equals zero," I replied. "What do you think about that?"

I handed him back the money, kissed my mother and little sister goodbye, and walked away....

I lay my head on the surfboard, and tried to relax. I heard Seth strumming a slow, thought-provoking melody on his acoustic guitar, music blending with the aspen wind, the flapping water, and the far-off sound of ski boats. The melody struck a promising chord as it fused with the pristine elements. But the water was getting very cold.

I dug in with my arms and propelled the surfboard back in

to lounge with Bandit, on a weathered, toasty-warm pier, jutting out from the continuous ring of evergreens and granite, which surround and shelter Lake Tahoe.

*   *   *

We parked where the road dead-ended. Zoe and I located the trailhead and started hiking along the path. According to the directions the owner had given Zoe, we were to follow the bank of the Truckee River through about fifty yards of dense forest; then we would reach a lone cabin.

Zoe had finally found us a place to live.

"It isn't large or fancy," she said, mimicking the voice of our new landlord. "Built it myself back in 1953. You could buy land on the Truckee for peanuts then."

She was quite pleased with herself—rightly so, I guessed. She had negotiated a very good price—and what was more, the cabin's owner lived down in Sacramento, so he wouldn't be around to bug us.

Our feet crunched dry pine needles. Zoe kept talking: "He then asked me, rather protectively, why I wanted to rent his place. I lied! This is great! I said we were a group of post-docs from Stanford University, who intended to co-op in Tahoe and study pollution and its effect on aquatic life such as trout."

"Sounds fascinating," she mimicked in a deep voice. "I recently retired from the State Department of Biology. I'm very interested in blue jays."

Zoe burst out laughing, "...and I replied, ha ha, oh my, 'now that is a real *Cyanocitta stelleri* for you.'"

I didn't have a clue what she was talking about.

"Family and Species of the bird. Steller's jay. Don't you see? Ha ha, oh my," she clarified. "After that, Danny, he lowered the rent even more. To *just peanuts*."

"Where did you pick up that *Cyanocitta stelleri* stuff?" I asked.

"From a handout in the Ranger Station," Zoe said in a breezy tone. "I'm rather fond of blue jays myself."

"Really?" I said.

"Really," she said.

Zoe Cleopatra Hash had no plans to diminish her studies in Tahoe.

*　　*　　*

The cabin standing before us was small and weathered. Yet nestled among the pines, on the rocky, granite bank of the Truckee, the dilapidated little cabin exhibited an unmistakable charm.

Abbey, Jay, and Seth had lagged behind, because Abbey had lost one of her army boots in the pile of gear and clothing in Jay's van. She insisted that she must wear her army boots if she was going to have to hike. The others were just now joining Zoe and me in front of the cabin.

"Look at those shutters and little Tyrolean things," Abbey said. She was a dazzling sight in her daringly short jean cutoffs and hefty black boots.

Zoe took the key out of her briefcase and we stepped inside. The cabin smelled of burnt wood and dampness. We switched on a light. We saw a beat-up old couch, some curious-looking chairs, and a rustic stone fireplace. Cobwebs and dust were also exposed, as well as a bunch of amateurish paintings of blue jays, arranged above the fireplace mantle.

"I dig the skis," Jay said of a pair of old wooden skis on the wall next to a pair of old-fashioned snowshoes, with webbing made from a crisscross of animal gut.

"Disgusting," Abbey called from the tiny kitchen. "There's mouse turds all over the counters."

"Oh my," echoed Zoe. "I have on sandals. Do you see any live ones?"

Downstairs consisted of a main room, kitchen, one small

bedroom, and a bath. Jay, Seth, and I explored the upstairs and discovered two sleeping lofts. There were twice as many spider webs upstairs. Seth found a clarinet stashed in a cardboard box underneath one of the beds. Jay thumbed through a pile of old *National Geographics*. "Tits, dude," he said, shoving a picture of an African woman in my face.

Abbey and Zoe put dibs on the bedroom downstairs.

Jay and I would bunk in one of the lofts upstairs.

Seth would occupy the other alone, since he snored.

The cabin had no phone, no water heater. But the stove worked. The toilet worked. Plenty of cold water sprayed out the shower. With a little work we knew we could fix up this place. Its remote location was perfect for practicing. Everyone agreed the cabin was 2001 times better than camping in the pickup and van.

Abbey immediately thought of a name for our wooden cabin. She called it Oz, because it was so much like a "fairy tale" and "so very, very serene."

*   *   *

I, personally, invited Abbey to go out on the town with Jay and me. But she, Zoe, and Seth were busy enjoying the cabin. Much to Zoe's pleasure, the landlord kept a small library of books downstairs; upon finding this, she immediately arranged the books alphabetically, by author. She was currently browsing through the collection, making a list of which books she intended to read and by when. That evening Seth was busy at the hearth branding the name "Oz" onto a wedge of pine. Abbey was killing spiders with a rolled-up newspaper. She dawned a quizzical expression, "I'd give my eyeteeth for a big, fat beanbag chair to put in front of the fireplace. And, no, Danny. I don't want to go anywhere tonight."

She had moved the knickknacks around on the fireplace mantel; re-hung and tried to better arrange the landlord's inherently awful collection of painted blue jays; even added things of her own to the decor, such as candles from Izy's shop, old flyers from club gigs in San Luis Obispo, and ashtrays she had stolen from the casinos.

As Jay and I went out the door, the girls dropped what they were doing and trailed behind us, with leftover spaghetti and vegetable pieces for the forest animals who came in the night. As Jay and I walked along the dark path toward the road where my truck and the van were parked, we heard the girls shriek, "Look, look, a squirrel! He's eating the spaghetti!"

*   *   *

According to our new manager, Zoe, nearby Tahoe City contained a variety of nightclubs. Jay and I decided to skip the dives and first check out what was reputed to be the big daddy. But first we stopped at a supermarket and bought a six-pack, so we could get a preliminary buzz on cheaply, before having to order drinks from an expensive bar.

When we got to the Lake Club, it was lit up like the casinos on the Nevada-side of the lake. The parking lots on both sides of the club were packed full of cars. I started to search for an empty slot but was stopped by a valet wearing a monkey suit. The jerk wanted two dollars to park my truck. I flipped a "U" and found a place alongside the main road a couple hundred yards down. Jay and I drank the six'er and got high.

A muscle-bound guy dressed in black greeted us at the entrance. "It's crowded tonight. Who are you guys?" His voice was as broad and muscled as his chest.

Jay said, "I'm the Nowhere Man. Is that cool or what?"

"You donkey," I said.

"We're at max capacity," said the doorman. "You gotta be on the list to get in."

"We're in a band," I said.

"Give me some names or buzz off, guys."

"I'm Danny Vikker and this is—"

"Blue Jay Wong."

"You donkey," I repeated.

The doorman checked his list and held out his hand like a policeman stopping traffic. "Sorry, guys. See you later."

"Try Zoe Cleopatra Hash," I said quickly. "That's our manager's name."

"Wait," he said. "Maybe."

Pretty soon, two couples walked out of the club and the bouncer nodded his head and said, "That will be five dollars each, gentlemen."

"Ouch," I said.

Jay and I fumbled for our wallets.

We passed through the double doors. "Bitchin', dude," said Jay. I realized, at once, that this was where Bandit *had* to play.

We gaped at the club's fantastic interior, its clean, angular architecture of parallel, perpendicular, skewed, and intersecting lines. Chrome trimming splayed lasers of colored light onto glossy white walls, cut-outs, and pillars. Bizarre art pieces and free-form metal statues sprang from the main floor like leafless trees. Some artist owning a cutting torch and a welder had gone wild. Music blasted from speakers everywhere; sleek, tan customers talked all at once.

There were no vacant tables and no empty stools at the downstairs bar. Jay and I climbed a flight of stairs leading to the upper level, centerless in construction, a catwalk bolted to the club's high walls. The catwalk connected a series of terraces with tables. Chrome chain-link fence caged in the walkway.

Jay and I found two empty seats on a terrace and sat down. We peered through the chrome mesh at a tangle of faces and bodies below, chopped into diamonds. It was half past nine. The band was due onstage at ten o'clock.

A cocktail waitress appeared before us, an extremely well-endowed blonde wearing a spandex tunic.

"Can I help you gents?" she asked with a European accent. Her voice sounded carefully polite, also tired.

Jay blatantly examined her from tip to toe. "What's your name, Total Babe?" he asked, his smile cracked wide, exposing his silver eye teeth.

The waitress ignored him and pulled out her ordering pad from a pocket in her micro apron. "I'm serious," Jay said. "You really are a Total Babe."

"He's wasted," I said.

The waitress petulantly clicked her tongue. "You're staring at my titties. Do you mind?"

Embarrassment turned Jay's face to putty.

She readied her pencil, "There's a two-drink minimum, gents. What'll you have?"

"Sorry for being a donkey," Jay said.

"Yes, our apologies for being rude," I said in my most chivalrous voice.

She smiled slightly. "These outfits they make us wear are a bloody pain."

She soon brought us a couple beers, took our precious money, and told Jay, much to my chagrin, that her name was Sly Michael and that she thought *he* was kind of dashing when he behaved himself.

I decided to go downstairs and dance until they shut off the canned music and the band came on.

I dodged elbows, brushed by stunning young women, swam through the crowd. A song by Tom Petty and the Heartbreakers blasted out of the circle of speakers on the main floor. My mind, however, was locked on an old Beatles tune, "Eleanor Rigby"—look at all the beautiful people—here, by God, is where they belong....

Expensive clothes. Honed gestures. The beam of confidence that comes from money. Everything about this club, everyone in this club, was so *very, very* chic.

I asked several young women to dance. One after another, they turned me down. My thrill for the Lake Club numbed. I was sixteen again, my father's country club, my first debutante ball.

Mary Lewis was beautiful. The bass line throbbed as we slow danced. Her hair smelled like velvet. Her body steamed. Electric skin....

"Dr. Lewis' daughter complained about you, Danny. She said you had an erection and were rubbing yourself against her leg when you were dancing with her.

"Christ, Danny. Jerry Lewis is a partner in my family practice. Jerry's a good guy—he laughed it off, but Mrs. Lewis and Mary—. Goddamn crap, it's an unqualified embarrassment that my only son is such a loser with girls. They think you're strange, Danny. Get with the program...."

"Excuse me." I stepped back. A girl in a red leather mini-skirt pushed by me.

I do all friggin' right with girls, I rationalized. So far in college I'd laid eleven different girls. After hanging around with Jay, I was getting good at picking up groupie chicks. But classy girls like Mary Lewis didn't like me. I'd never even put my arm around Abbey Butler.

I went back upstairs, intent on getting shit-faced and checking out some Tahoe rock 'n' roll—maybe steal some licks for Bandit. If we got a gig here, perhaps my luck would change....

*   *   *

The Pronouns were quite a spectacle. The band had five members. All of them, including the girl, had the new eighties-style haircuts—short on top, long in the back, with pointed Star Trek sideburns. Each member wore black trousers and boots, and a jersey bearing his or her stage name. "He" played guitar. "She" sang. "Them" played bass. "It" sat behind the drums. "Us" played synthesizer.

"He" and "She" fronted the band. "He," wearing his personalized jersey cut down with scissors to the size of a bra, was doing half of his guitar playing with his butt turned to the audience. As he shook his butt back and forth, he cocked his neck to one side, and gave his face to the audience—his nose crinkled, his eyes and mouth opened painfully wide as if by toothpicks. While "She" was singing her heart out, she continually ran her fingers through her black, stringy hair. When she wasn't doing this, she ran her hands up and down her hips. "She" had a rough look, and growled and sneered. "She" was also about twenty pounds overweight. But, as much as I hated to admit it, the Mr. and Mrs. of the Pronouns had definite talent. "He" played a mean guitar, and "She" had a clear, gutsy voice, which in some ways reminded me of Abbey's.

The bassist, "Them," was a tall black guy with a small head and long neck. Jay, who normally wasn't as critical of people as I was, said, "That fuckin' bassist looks like a rooster." "Them" stood motionless as he played, except for his long fingers, which seemed to move on the bass strings weightlessly, like ripples on water. Out of the neckline of "Them's" jersey protruded a white, Nehru collar. Very spiritual, man.

The keyboard player, "Us," was equally as laid-back and wore dark sunglasses like Ray Charles, only "Us" didn't smile or rock his head from side to side when he played. He was dead still.

The drummer was pudgy like the singer and equally as wild. "It" looked like an *it* as he threw himself around his drum set hitting the heads harder than Keith Moon. But "It" played a perfectly solid beat. I couldn't argue with that.

As Jay and I listened jealously to the Pronouns, Sly frequently passed by our table. Jay and I couldn't help but order more beers, and soon we were broke. Jay conned Sly into bringing us the rest of our beers for free. Jay and I became increasingly heated, and the voluptuous wiggles of the girls on the dance floor looked better and better. I was still too intimidated to ask one of them to dance.

"Bitchin'," Jay said. He must have said the word "bitchin'" about three million times that night.

I hit the john when the band went on break and bumped into "He." The guitarist was drying his underarms with the electric blower on the wall, cool and nonchalant about it.

"I play in a band, too," I said. "We just came to Tahoe. We're looking for work."

"He" started blow-drying his neck, cocking it the same way he did when he did his little number onstage. "And you are?"

"Bandit."

"Never heard of you."

"You will," I said. "Your guitar sounds hot tonight."

"Don't kiss my ass," he said.

I wasn't surprised to see that his ass was pointing in my direction.

"You want free advice?" he continued. "Here it is: You aren't going to get a job here. This is *the* place, and *the* place doesn't hire scrub bands. The end."

"Nice story," I said.

"What do you play, anyway?"

"Drums," I said.

"I should have guessed," he said.

The asshole left.

I wondered what the hell he had against drummers. I appraised myself in the mirror. I saw: The lean frame and red cheeks of an English-American. Brown hair that was getting longer and longer. My friggin' pug nose.

I looked deeply into the reflection of my eyes. My eyes looked weird like a zoo monkey's. Curious, afraid, pathetic, bulging…. I realized that I was incredibly drunk and let out a huge, roguish beer belch.

Back at our table, on the cage-like terraces on the catwalk

surrounded by chrome chain-link fence, Jay was rapping with Sly. She was sitting in my seat. "Goodness, I'd better hop back to it." She began taking orders at another table.

"Sorry to scare her away," I said to Jay.

Jay pushed yet another beer toward me. "Listen, dude, Sly said this place is happening outside, too. Let's check out the dock." He chugged his beer and motioned for me to do the same.

"Fuckin' cheers," I said.

Floodlights lined the backside of the club. There were quite a few boats moored to the private deck and landing. Most of the crafts were hot ski boats. I watched the rhythm of the boats, bobbing gently on ripples caused by the faint pull of the moon, and the nighttime breeze.

Only a handful of patrons were gathered on the deck, couples chipped off from the crowd inside. The action Sly spoke of didn't exist—at least not at that select moment.

Jay and I dangled our feet off the end of the main pier. The soles of our shoes barely scraped the water. The Tahoe air was hinted with the smell of pine trees, smoke, and trout. You could look up and see every star in the sky embedded in blackness. If you looked straight ahead, the night over the water appeared infinite in expanse.

Darkness grabbed my mind and pulled it down, down— into the depths of the cold, dark liquid. I imagined myself naked in the liquid darkness and shivering; yet strangely, I could breathe. Then I turned into liquid myself, a formless fluttering meniscus, like a dollop of oil. This was always the beginning of my dreams about Tahoe.

A string of red, green, and amber lights appeared in the darkness stretching beyond the pier. We heard the sound of a boat.

As the craft approached, the bow light became brighter and brighter. We had to crinkle our eyes. The pilot kept gunning the peppy engine. *Varuum, glug, glug, glug, varuum.* The image of a large inboard ski boat and its captain and passengers materialized. The pilot looked about our age. The three girls with him looked younger.

"You want to earn yourselves a beer?" the pilot called to Jay and me. He threw us the bow line and scurried to the front of the boat to assist us; he seemed intent upon making this a perfect landing. He instructed me to hold the bow line while he hung rubber bumpers from the side. He then threw a line from the stern to Jay.

"Don't haul it in yet," he told Jay. "You," he said to me, "be more careful. I don't want the bow to get scratched."

He leapt from the boat to the dock and ousted Jay from his job of securing the stern. He precisely tied the rear line to a cleat on the dock, and yanked on the knot to make sure it was taut. He then shooed me away from the bow, untying my knot and re-tying the bow line his way. "Well done," he said to Jay and me.

Remaining genuinely enthused, he introduced himself as "Edward Mason, Jr." and said he was eager to have that beer with us as soon as we unloaded the passengers. The passengers included his younger sister, "Tish," and her friends, "Rhonda" and "Manny."

Edward was slim with reddish-brown hair and a freckled complexion. His preppy attire included a thick cashmere sweater and deck shoes like Zoe's. His face was rather plain and boyish. The three young girls had faces that were much more striking. The girls wore lots of makeup, lots of jewelry, and short, slinky, sparkly dresses that showed off their creamy, tanned skin.

We helped the girls onto the dock. The girls were as bossy as Eddy; unlike Eddy, however, they were not interested in drinking beer on the dock with us.

As the three girls started toward the club, Tish said, "Manny, you said you were going to borrow your sister's I.D.

Tell me, what do you want *us* to *do*, if they don't let you in?"

Little Manny crooned, "Oh *stifle*, Tishy. I know that big apey bouncer. He lets me in *all* the time."

"My father *told* him to," added Rhonda.

We watched them push through the back door without being questioned.

"Girls," Edward mused.

"Women," I mused.

"I've got plenty of beer on ice," he continued. "Be prepared, that's what I always say." Eddy accented his last statement with a clean, orthodontic smile.

He instructed Jay and me to board his boat, the *Blue Max* as the bow read. He cautioned us about stepping on the chrome railing as we hopped in.

Eddy told us he was living in his parents' summer house on the lake, and that his parents were in Japan. "Anyway, I think that's where they are," he continued. "They travel quite a lot, you know." It came out in the conversation that Eddy was thirty years old, which surprised me. He looked much younger.

"What do you do for a living, Eddy?" I asked.

"Nothing," Eddy said. "I'm rich."

"Sounds pretty all right," Jay said.

Eddy replied, "It is and it isn't. Being rich has its good and bad points."

"Good God, what the hell could be bad about it?" I asked.

Eddy got himself another beer and didn't answer my question; instead he invited us to a late-night party at his place, after the club shut down at two o'clock. Bragging, I told Eddy that Jay and I were up for anything, because our schedule was flexible. We were rock musicians.

"Really?" Eddy said. "I love music. I'm impressed. Let me buy you two another round inside." I felt guilty that I had neglected to tell Eddy also that we were out-of-work rock musicians.

Chaperoned by Eddy, all of a sudden Jay and I lost our outlaw status and became a part of the clique scene at the Lake Club. Eddy knew tons of people. We joined his sister, Tish, who sat with her girlfriends at a table next to the dance floor. It was the Pronoun's last set, and they were playing very loudly. In order for someone to hear you talk, you had to yell. I asked Tish to dance, and she said, "Yes." She and her girlfriends became very friendly toward Jay and me. I found myself having a blast. All too soon, the Pronouns ended their show, and bright lights flicked on inside the club. Eddy, Tish, and her friends left for the marina. I looked around the main floor for Jay.

As the crowd poured out the front and back, the Lake Club opened up and became like a solemn gallery. The blow-torch statues—the sharp-edged rusty metal—began to give me the creeps. Jay finally reappeared.

He grinned from ear to ear. "Hey, dude, that chick, Sly, is taking me home with her," he said.

"You donkey. How'd you pull that off?"

"She gave me some bullshit about going over to her place for a nightcap. I told her I didn't have a car. She said we could worry about that later. I think she's horny, dude."

"I think you're right," I said somberly. I told him to have a good time.

"Cheer up, man," Jay said. "You going over to Eddy's?"

"I don't know."

It was a lonely business to be stuck solo after drinking and looking at women all friggin' night long. I started having some wild ideas about going back to the cabin, and waking up Abbey, trying to put a move on her. But I knew I wasn't friggin' good enough yet. Paradiddle. Paradiddle.

I stumbled into a bulletin board, mounted to an A-frame stand in the lobby. I leaned against it, trying to take a breather. The friggin' flimsy stand nearly toppled over. I fixed the stand.

My eyes scanned over blurry newsprint. Then, this one flyer

went off like a bomb: "Appearing Labor Day Weekend. Three nights only. L.A.'s hottest new group, the Pricey Dexters."

Man oh man, I couldn't even deal with this. It was too much, *too much*. I let the bad news dissolve in my pickled brain, until Domino's coming to Tahoe was comical. What the hell, I thought, I'm drunk off my ass. *What the hell*. Dumb laughs trickled out of my numb mouth. *Crap, Danny. I say crap, you loser.*

I ran back through the club to the decking, down the stairs to the dock. I yelled to Eddy, "You still *hav'n* that *par-tee? I's really fucked up, buddy.*" It looked like a few extra people besides Tish and company were in Eddy's boat.

"Yeah, sure, a bunch of people are coming over," Eddy said impatiently. "We're casting off. Come on."

I didn't care who the hell was going to be there. My dumb laugh started again...*loser*.... I scurried aboard the *Blue Max*. Varuum. Glug. Glug.

We headed onto the lake, bled into darkness.

Chapter 7
Pihtahbah Pihtahbah

My head felt like it was stuffed with cotton, and it was sure good to be back at the cabin—back at Oz as the front door now read, thanks to Seth's handiwork.

I had to concentrate hard to put into focus some of the events that took place at Eddy's lake house. I remembered our arrival clearly. Sitting at the wheel of the Blue Max, Eddy pulled out a small plastic box and pushed a button. A big metal door rolled up slowly, whining from rust like a draw bridge. Eddy shifted the motor out of neutral and roared his ski boat into a boat garage that hovered over the lake like a barn.

Once inside, he told his guests, "I've got stuff for sale, if anyone is interested." I didn't have a dime left after the Lake Club, but Eddy was pretty generous and cut lines of coke for everyone to sample, and Eddy's idea of a sample was enough to make my ears sweat. The Pronoun's bassist and keyboard player, "Us" and "Them," were present. I remember "Us" passing Eddy a wad of cash for a big buy. "Us" and "Them" split after that. Including Tish and her friends, there were about twenty-five guests partying with Eddy at his parents' decadent lake house.

After seeing the flyer announcing the upcoming arrival of Domino and the Pricey Dexters, and after walking out of the Lake Club solo, I felt like getting even more obliterated. People kept turning me onto lines, and I kept wetting my dry, numb throat with alcohol. The stereo blasted Tom Petty and the Heartbreakers. I remember Petty's scratchy, acrimonious voice repeatedly singing out the chorus: "She's a woman in love, love, love…. She's a woman in love, love, love…and it's not me." I remember I felt like snatching the record off the turntable and hurling it out into the big, cold lake.

Things started spinning and coming out of alignment. I left Eddy's giant party room with its hardwood bar and expensive everything, and climbed a spiral staircase. The stairs made me more dizzy. I stumbled around upstairs and tried to find a place to lie down. Somebody's hand squeezed mine.

"Are you okay? You look pretty messed up," Tish said.

"Fine, thank you," I said. It was excruciatingly difficult to try and compose myself. "I decided to take a little tour. I'm fine, thank you. Nice pace—. I mean place." Dumb laughter started trickling out of my mouth like syrup. "Oh man, man, man. I'm so fucked up," I said.

Tish thought this was funny. "*Ooooh*. I like the last part," she said.

"Do you want to know a secret?"

"Pretty please."

"I like the last part, too."

"Danny, what do you mean?"

"Hey, wait a minute."

"A minute? I hope it takes longer than that."

"Longer?"

"Yes, longer. *Ooooh*."

Deep inside, a small part of me remained sober; this part, my good fairy, reprimanded me for flirting with Tish, who was certainly old enough in mind and body for sex but whose legal age, I feared, was not greater-than-or-equal-to the statutory limit. My good fairy also blessed me with a sliver of equilibrium and kept me from throwing up. Thank you, good fairy. Unfortunately, my good fairy's words of wisdom about Tish were spoken in a very faint voice and were easy to ignore.

We stood in a bedroom with a king-size waterbed. Built into the wall above the bed was a 100-gallon aquarium full of turtles and gold fish.

"Your pets?" I asked.

"Yeah," she replied.

"Hey," I said. "Why don't we feed them some fish food. I like to watch fish eat."

"I can think of something a lot more interesting to do than that," Tish said.

So much for talking innocently about gold fish and turtles. Sorry, good fairy.

Tish stripped down to bikini panties and a petite lacy bra. She lay down on her waterbed and invited me to join her. Still buzzed and sluggish, I moved on top of her; she kissed me wetly and arched so that her groin collided with mine. It felt like I was in slow motion compared with her. Then, I sped up and she slowed down, until our crotches—still separated by a thin layer of moist cloth—ground together in a matched rhythm. I tore away her panties. She told me to wait.

Before I could enter her, she made me sprinkle her clitoris with cocaine and lick it off. The coke made the salty stink between her legs taste pure and clean. Also, the coke made saliva pour out of my mouth. As we made it, I thought of *coming—coming* in her, *coming* all over her. I felt like a male animal going after a female animal in heat.

When I awoke, I thought of *going*. But it was she who was gone.

"At the beach, so thanks for last night. See ya around," the note read, in the large curly-cue handwriting of a girl. It was signed "Tishy," and at the bottom of the note there was a sketch of a Happy Face, changed so that the mouth was drawn with an "O" rather than a wide "U." She also made one of Happy Face's eyes a line rather than a dot, so that he was winking. A bubble above the face made the cartoon say, "Nummy-num-num."

"So you wound up with dear Tishy," Eddy said, as he prepared a thermos of coffee for the boat ride back to the Lake Club and my pickup. He looked disgusted. I didn't blame him.

If it would have been my sister, I would have been furious.

"Sorry, Eddy," I said, feeling like a jerk. "I didn't know what I was doing last night. Hey, I'll talk to her and stop things."

He brushed off my apology. "Talk to her?" he said. "She and her friends are the biggest sluts in Tahoe. She screws everybody." He paused. "I guess I'm not the greatest moral influence on her."

"What can you do?" I said.

"Nothing, I just hope she doesn't get knocked up or get herpes or something. At least I was straight when I was in high school. When I went to Yale, I just drank. Now it's a different story. But I have to give myself credit for then."

I said, "Sure, Eddy. Can you give me that ride now?"

He fixed us both a Bloody Mary for our hangovers. "Cheers," he said.

By the time I got out of there I was feeling like a total degenerate. I sought relief back at Oz. I needed to practice my drums.

*　　*　　*

Right-left-right-left. I tested my snare and it snapped back with the sound "Pit-Pit-Pit-Pit."

Left-left. I struck the small tom and heard a throaty response, "Tom-Tom."

"Chink-Chink" went the hi-hat, and "Ding-Ding" went the ride cymbal.

My right foot tested the bass drum. "Bugg. Bugg-Bugg-Bugg." I loved my drum set's bass drum; it had an especially thick sound, like a mallet hitting a side of beef.

I decided to work on triplets. "It" of the Pronouns had done a nice series of them in his drum solo. I set my metronome on 160 and counted along a couple measures, "one-two-three-four, two-two-three-four." I played one *tri-po-let* slowly, "Pit. Tom. Bugg." Then faster, "Pit-tom-bugg." Then *a tempo* for a measure, "Pihtahbah-Pihtahbah-Pihtahbah-Pihtahbah." And for another, "Pihtahbah-Pihtahbah-Pihtahbah-Pihtahbah."

Then *a tempo* measure after measure. "Pihtahbah-Pihtahbah-Pihtahbah-Pihtahbah. Pihtahbah-Pihtahbah-Pihtahbah-Pihtahbah. Pihtahbah-Pihtahbah-Pihtahbah-Pihtahbah. Pihtahbah-Pihtahbah-Pihtahbah-Pihtahbah."

I experimented, working in other drums. A roto tom-tom-bass triplet made the sound "Tootahbah." Other variations produced "Tahpihbah" and "Bahtahpih." The possibilities of this lick were endless. I played until my hands and feet were tired.

"Don't stop on account of us," said Abbey, who was sitting on the fireplace hearth reading the latest issue of *People* magazine. On the front cover was a portrait of Lady Di, soon-to-be Princess of England. Zoe sat nearby at the small, rickety table she used as a desk, when the rest of us weren't eating off it. Positioned in front of her was her open briefcase.

"Your drums have been sounding really tight lately." Abbey turned the page of her magazine. Her green eyes remained focused downward on glitzy pictures and gossip. "I'm an expert on drums, and drummers, you know," she added.

I didn't reply. I was no longer so pleased that she was pleased with my drumming.

Zoe had bright news, at least. She had found Bandit a job at a place called the Hofbrau. It was a steady gig, five nights a week, Tuesday through Saturday. She was currently drawing up a contract and this activity seemed to amuse her very much. "You wouldn't believe the list of stipulations I've come up with," she said brightly. "The nitty gritty details of business can be absolutely rigorous." She adjusted her professorial glasses.

Abbey chuckled from behind the pages of *People*.

It annoyed me that Abbey was so interested in garbage like Lady Di's famous new hairdo and her upcoming plans for holy matrimony to that big-eared polo player, Prince Charles. A friggin' match made in heaven, as far as I was concerned.

I sat down next to Abbey at the hearth. "What do you think of Lady Di's haircut?" I said flatly.

"If she wants to look like a page boy, that's her prerogative. God, but to think of it. Di's going to be sssooo rich." She paused. "Why should you care?"

"Just making conversation."

She reached over and ruffled my hair. "Danny, you're such a sweet little bird sometimes."

I forgave her for everything.

Her expression turned sad. "Actually—, I just started reading about something else. There's a follow-up on that fellow who shot John."

She flipped backward a couple of pages and located a line with her index finger. "'It was almost as if I was on some kind of special mission that I could not avoid....' That's Mark Chapman's excuse. Can you believe it? He wants people to think he's special."

"He's a psycho," I said. "What do you expect?"

"Don't be flip. Doesn't this bother you?"

"Yes."

"You know what I think? I think they ought to hang him by his prick."

"Abbey!" Zoe interjected, from across the room. "That would be inhumane."

"Justice is sometimes inhumane," she told her spiritual sister. "Don't be such an idealist."

"I like being an idealist." Zoe went back to her papers.

"And another thing," Abbey said, "have you read this book *Catcher in the Rye*?"

"Sure," I said.

"Hasn't everybody?" Zoe said.

"I haven't," Abbey said. "I was supposed to one time, but I read something else instead."

"You should read it," Zoe said. "It's a very engaging novel.

There's this boy, Holden Caulfield, who's rather a smart aleck. Oh my, it's sad. Holden has a dead brother named Allie, and poor Holden thinks about him all the time. What's curious, you see, about Allie is that he used to write poetry on his baseball mitt...."

Abbey spoke quickly, before Zoe had the chance to launch into a critical literary discussion of J.D. Salinger. "The point is, it says here that Chapman thought he was that guy in the book, Holden Caulfield."

"That's correct," Zoe said. "So?"

"I think Holden is cool," I said.

"The point I'm trying to make is that Mark Chapman is *absolutely crazy.* It scares me to think there are people like that in this world." She tossed the magazine aside and sprawled, face down, on the floor. She laced her fingers into the brown hair covering her ears.

Zoe came over and sat next to me on the hearth. We both looked down at Abbey. My back felt cold. There was no fire in the fireplace.

"Aren't you being a little melodramatic, Abbey?" Zoe asked. Abbey said nothing. No one spoke after that.

When John Lennon was a Beatle, I was a preadolescent, too young to understand Lennon's political and social messages. I was then under the impression that there was an abundance of Peace and Love in the world, not a shortage. I didn't have a clue what the songs meant.

But every radio station played the Beatles. I grew up listening to their music in the background, and liked it much for the same reason that I liked Disneyland: the songs' colorful places and funny characters captured my imagination.

Yellow submarines, eggmen, kites, diamonds, marmalade skies, meter maids, strawberry fields, walruses, nowhere, everywhere, revolution, Rocky Raccoon, Sgt. Pepper, Penny Lane....

Now, as I sat in the cabin called Oz looking down at Abbey,

bits and pieces of Beatles songs swam once again in my mind. I felt like I did when I was a young boy. I realized how awful it was that someone had killed John Lennon.

We put on a couple Beatles records and listened to them reverently.

*   *   *

"I'm still depressed," Abbey said. "I'm going for a walk." She pulled her army boots over the bottoms of her jeans. The jeans clung tightly to her small calves and narrow ankles and showed off her legs handsomely. "Anyone care to join me?"

"I'm busy," Zoe said.

Abbey opened the door. Green incense rushed into the cabin, as did the sound of the churning Truckee River. "Come on, Danny," she said. "I need some company."

Here's my chance to impress her, I thought—but once I was outside, alone with her, I was speechless.

"Cat got your tongue?" she teased.

"Cat? No," I said.

"You're weird, Danny."

Loser…crap…Mary Lewis said…Perverted.…

What the hell was my problem? The only women I had success with were promiscuous groupies and teenage nymphos. This was easy. They made all the moves.

I didn't know how to go after a real woman, like Abbey. I just didn't have the guts.

*   *   *

When I was fourteen I had a hernia operation. A pretty brunette nurse came into the room to shave me before I went on the table. I was red-faced, embarrassed, and desperately trying to stave off an erection while her hands worked around my genitals. I kept having this fantasy about the nurse drawing the curtains around my hospital bed, removing her white nylons, pulling up her crisp white dress, climbing on top of me, and moaning in rapture as she moved up and down. I had read about such wonderful occurrences in men's magazines. There was this guy at my high school who claimed something like this had happened to him—while he was at the chiropractor, an exotic Japanese nurse gave him a blowjob.

I couldn't control myself. The pretty brunette nurse smiled patiently, not seeming alarmed. She bowed her middle finger against her thumb, and snapped the finger hard against the underside of my erection—instantly yielding smallness, softness, and a stinging welt. "Don't be ashamed. I have to do that a lot," she said, "even with adult men, sometimes." She finished shaving me and scrubbed me raw with yellow pre-op disinfectant.

*   *   *

I thought about that friggin' nurse as Abbey and I strolled through the forest. Abbey Butler was equally deft at "snapping" guys when the need arose. But soon I discovered Abbey wasn't acting like that nurse at all.

We walked slowly along the narrow path that followed the river, our shoulders brushing together. We traveled in the same direction that the river flowed, downstream from Oz. The woods grew thicker and more lush, and the path became more cluttered with pine needles and twigs. Abbey ran ahead.

"Look at all of the lovely pinecones," she called back to me. "I'm going to find one that's just perfect and box it up and send it to Izy." I continued walking until I caught up with her. She stood holding a fine pinecone. Our eyes met and locked.

"I think your mother will really like that," I said.

We located a large granite rock on the edge of the Truckee and climbed onto it. "It's getting cold," she said. "Do you mind?" She snuggled against me, as we sat looking down at the water. Her body felt soft and warm.

"Danny," she exclaimed, "we've found Oz. We're living in

Oz." Her eyes remained fixed upon the rapids. "Life is being so good to me lately," she said. "Not too long ago, a lot of things were wrong. I feel so very happy right now."

The thin mountain air seemed to amplify the sounds of the forest—the rustle of squirrels and creatures, the rush of clear liquid over rocks, the creaking and cracking of wood. In the deep forest, our voices sounded crisp and chimy like brass bells.

"I feel very happy right now, too," I said. "And it's because of you."

"Do you think so?" Abbey said coyly. "Is it because of me? Or is it because of this pretty forest?"

"Because of you," I said.

"Not this?" she asked.

"That's right," I said.

"Well," she said, "since I'm in too good of a mood to give you a hard time, I'll say thank you. But just because I feel so sweet, don't take it for granted." She tilted her head, laughed.

"What was wrong with your life?" I asked.

"Oh, a lot," she said.

"Tell me about Domino."

Abbey studied my face. She seemed to be trying to decide whether or not she wanted to answer. She took a deep breath, the same way she did before she sang a long note. "Everyone knows I used to go out with Bandit's old drummer," she said. "But, you see, I really loved him. It wasn't like me at all. It's more fun to like guys just a little. Then, if you need to, you can be mean to them." She rolled the pinecone she had picked up for Isabella, over and over, spinning it backwards, into herself, as if it were the mechanism of a clock, unwinding.

"So much happened between Domino and me. I can't tell you everything. I don't want to tell you everything." She looked up from the spinning pinecone. "You probably think I'm pretty sure of myself, don't you?"

"Yes," I said.

Abbey sighed.

"Oh Danny," she said, "it seems like a long time ago. I moved away from Izy and joined Bandit. It was back when I met Zoe, and Domino. San Luis Obispo was kind of like our little Oz is now. At first there weren't any jobs, but there seemed to be so much promise. Eventually we made it. We became popular! Then, things blew up."

She tossed her pinecone into the water, and it floated away. The feisty Abbey spoke. "It was all such a fucking mess. I never felt so much pain." She started to cry, yet before she became lost in emotion she stopped herself.

She dried her eyes on the sleeve of her jacket, and we listened to the forest sounds. A blue jay squawked nearby. The jay woke us from the dream. "You have your arm around me," she said. "I just realized that."

The wicked snap. I withdrew the arm I had ever-so-gently placed around her.

"You don't have to do that," she said. "Why are you so timid? Do I scare you?"

"Sort of," I said.

"Haven't you figured it out by now?" Her ever-changing eyes were now the color of the halo of pine needles above her head. "I'm the one who's afraid. I know you care for me, Danny, but I don't like to admit that I care for you. You're such a coincidence, damn you."

We kissed. And I would remember it forever. The green, forest kiss of Oz.

When our lips parted, I felt like I was glued to the granite rock. Abbey was charged with energy, and she shot up and brushed the twigs off her jeans. "Can you help me now?" she asked. "I'd like to find another pinecone to send to Izy." Arm in arm, we sprung to the task, and Abbey hummed a song I had never before heard into the nape of my neck. What was happening didn't seem real.

*　　*　　*

In the days following our walk in the forest, Abbey continued to be affectionate with me, up to a point. We sat around together in the evenings and snuggled in front of the fire. We went on more walks, scavenged for pinecones, talked for hours. But the intimacy stopped at kisses. She told me she wanted things to happen slowly. I hadn't expected such caution from her, and it made her even more attractive.

One evening I drove her to a pay phone so she could call her mother. Standing outside the telephone booth, I could barely hear her voice. It was muffled, and the *whish-whish* of cars driving past the gas station on Tahoe City's main drag sometimes drowned out Abbey's voice completely. Yet, the last thing she told her mother before she clacked the resin-hard receiver into the hook was clear: "Tell Hector I love him. Mother, tell him I miss him a lot."

*　　*　　*

Bars smell funny. Especially in the morning when all the customers are home, and it's dead silent. The spilled beer in the carpet smells like sweet rotten rice. The counters smell like stale oil and stick to your elbows. It is said: take one of the five senses away and the other four become keener. In a bar in the morning, there's nothing to hear, to hug, to see among the dreary tables, to taste because the thought of liquor is about as appealing as the thought of drinking cough syrup. So the nose becomes kingpin and detects the residue of barf in the far corner, from the girl who drank ten daiquiris on her twenty-first birthday.

I got a bad impression of the Hofbrau the morning we set up. The place reeked. Now, as I ate my complimentary dinner before our first show, the Hofbrau still didn't impress me. There was a four-inch black hair baked into the meat of my hamburger. I would have gone to the rest room and made myself throw up, but I was afraid I might get stabbed.

Mickey, the manager, stood across from me. He was serving food and tending bar. I dangled the black hair in front of him, as though it were a piece of thread. Mickey laughed and remarked wryly, "Look at what the cat drug in. Ha. Ha. Hey, let me get ya another." He turned to the nearest waitress. "Who in hell's cooking back there? One of the guys in the band got some goddamn hair in his goddamn burger." Mickey shoved my plate into the young girl's hands, which were already full of empty mugs. "What the hell's his name? Oh yeah, Danny. Get Danny another one of these. And tell that dirt-ball to put on a hair net for Christ's sake!"

Treating me as if I were his good buddy, Mickey confided, "You wouldn't know the problems I have. The help I get is lousy. Plain lousy. Listen here, Danny, you guys do good tonight. Play some good music, okay?"

I never did get my second hamburger. My stomach was thankful.

That evening the Hofbrau swam with ruffian clientele. Burly men in T-shirts sporting boating murals and beer ads lounged loudly and heavily at the tables. Pool sharks circled the tables in back. Hard-looking women weaved in and out of the men, or sat among themselves and smoked cigarettes. The women's voices sounded like splintering wood. The men's voices sounded like a fleet of diesel trucks.

Abbey, Seth, Jay and Sly, and Zoe emerged from the back room. Abbey was heralded with cat-calls. She had on a tanktop with no bra, tight jeans, and snakeskin boots. Her face was painted wildly with stripes of blue and green eye shadow, red-red rouge, and red-red lipstick. Her boot heels snapped the floor like a whip.

"How do I look?" she said, spinning around for me. She was acting very giddy, full of artificial energy. So was Zoe.

"You look great," I told her. I wondered what the girls were on.

"Good," she exclaimed, giving me a firecracker kiss on the cheek. She let her lips remain next to my ear. "Be careful," she whispered. "Tonight might be your night."

I about fell off my barstool.

Abbey slipped me a couple of pink hearts.

Eddy had recently paid us a visit at the cabin and had brought us a jar full of uppers as a gift. Though it was no lake house, Eddy really liked our cabin called "Oz." One thing about Eddy, even though he was rich, he wasn't a snob. Eddy was kind of a bad influence, however. Groupies tended to be like that.

"This place is a dump," Abbey shrieked. "Let's get crazy. What the hell."

She announced to the audience that I, the drummer, would kick off the show, and for 32 measures I played variations of Pittahbah-Pittahbah-Pittahbah-Pittahbah. I cued Jay, and we kicked in the rest of the band. We did a couple originals by Seth, next a medley of old Stones songs, during which the place went wild.

Some bikers arrived during the second set, and Mickey cautioned us to ignore them. He said a couple of them played, and they were always wanting to jam with club bands. Jay broke a string, and while he changed it, one of the bikers approached me. He was tall as a lumberjack, and wore oily black leather and a long buck knife.

"I'd like to play your drums, pal," he said. He helped himself to one of my spare drumsticks and started testing my floor tom. He smelled like the underside of a junked Buick.

"Oh, you play drums?" I said nicely.

"No, I just want to make a fool out of myself. Fuck yes, I play."

"Nothing personal, but we like to keep it pretty professional onstage. Sorry about that."

"You're real funny. Real funny, ya know." The large biker smiled, and I saw that all of his teeth were rotten. "If you don't let me play, I'm gonna fuck you up. I'm going to fucking kill you."

"That's the magic word," I said. This friggin' moron pissed me off, but I wasn't going to provoke him into using his buck knife.

Seth and Abbey remained frozen. Jay shrugged and indicated his bass was ready. The biker was amused. "Guess what? I'm going to do you a favor," he said, pushing me back down onto my drummer's throne. "I don't think you really want me to play, and it fucking hurts my feelings. It fucking hurts my feelings like a little baby. You go ahead and play tonight, pal. You go ahead and don't say I never did nothing for you." The biker issued a few bullish snorts and left. The sonofabitch gave me the creeps.

For a while, the bikers behaved. Then a woman with tattoos got on one of the tables and did the writhing dance of a harem girl. The girl caught Abbey's eyes, and Abbey started rooting for the dumb slut between songs. Jay, who was also cranked on uppers, egged on the biker chick. The crowd grew around the table, and the woman shucked her top and started shaking her floppy white tits with large, cocoa-brown nipples. Mickey tried to stop the woman, but the bikers pushed him away.

The biker who hassled me about playing my drums climbed onto the table, took his shirt off, and started dancing an erotic duet with the woman. My biker friend kept yelling, "Booga-booga-booga!" as he stuck his face between the woman's tits. Each time he came up for air, he issued a goofy look to the crowd and everyone cheered. The tall biker was sloppy drunk and his long frame teetered on the table. We didn't know what to do, so we continued to play. Most of the dancers cleared the floor and gathered around the live, impromptu sex act.

An even bigger, meaner-looking biker—who was big like a gorilla as opposed to tall like a lumberjack—pulled my friend off the table. The big newcomer evidently wanted to sample the woman's tits for himself. The tall one made the mistake of pushing the big one back. The newcomer attacked the other viciously, throwing him down on the floor and kicking his stomach with thick-soled motorcycle boots. The big gorilla stopped, and the tall biker lay motionless.

Slowly, life returned. The tall one got up, bloody and lame, and limped away. "Fuck you," he cried shakily. "You can have the slut."

Human nature. The crowd sided with the big gorilla, and heckled the loser. Even the biker women were cruel. "Boo. Boo. Chicken-fucker. Chicken-fucker. He needs another lesson. Get him. Boo. Boo."

We gave up trying to play. Mickey was behind the bar on the phone. I hoped he was calling the cops.

I sensed what the stupid tall guy would do. In a rage, he unsheathed his buck knife and ran hog-wild at the big biker. But the gorilla broke a chair over the tall one's head before he could cut him. The knife slid onto the dance floor. Nobody touched it.

The big one climbed onto the tall one's chest and grabbed a fist-full of hair. He slammed the loser's head into the wood flooring. Before each slam, he lectured the senseless, bloody head. "Nobody fucks with me." Bash. "Nobody pulls a knife on me." Slam. "A brother who turns gots ta pay." Thud. "Nobody fucks with me." Crack.

The blade of the buck knife gleamed on the vacant dance floor like poison.

The cops cleared the place. Abbey, Zoe, and Sly were shaken up. They went in the back room and wouldn't come out. We put away the instruments.

"I wonder if that biker is dead," Jay mused, as he wiped down his bass.

"Close to it," I said.

"This place is strange," said Seth. He had just gone outside to watch the medics load the biker into the ambulance. Seth looked sick to his stomach.

"Strange? That's a real astute observation, dude," Jay said.

Seth lit a cigarette. He started several times to issue one of his famous polka-dotted party horn laughs. But he couldn't make himself get happy. "Shit," he said. "In addition to this place being a war zone, there's ghosts around here."

"Good God, what are you mumbling about?" I asked. I was in no mood for any of Seth's arty, spiritualistic bullshit. Neither was Jay. We wanted to get our stuff packed up and go home.

"No kidding, you two," Seth said testily, "I saw a car-load of guys drive by. They slowed down to look at the ambulance and shit. One of them looked just like Uwe."

"Too bad for that guy," said Jay.

"You think I'm crazy?" Seth said.

"So Uwe has a look-alike in Tahoe. What's the big deal?" I said.

Seth angrily snapped the latches on his guitar case. "Well maybe I don't like people's faces that look like Uwe's face, Danny. And fuck you, too, Jay."

"Mellow out," Jay said.

"Yeah, we're just kidding," I said. "Maybe it was Uwe. Who the hell knows?"

"I doubt it," Seth said.

"Yeah," said Jay, "Stranglehold's long-gone down in L.A., kissing the Man's heiny."

Seth lit another cigarette. "Where's the girls? I want to go back to the cabin. This gig is definitely over."

Far off in an echo chamber, I heard Abbey Butler's voice, affectionate and suggestive like it had been earlier in the evening before things got messy:

"Tonight…your night…tonight…your night.…"

Today had been very bad. Tomorrow, however, was looking better.

Chapter 8
Nightmares, Mushrooms, and Daytime Dreams

"The manager of the Lake Club is particular," Zoe Cleopatra Hash said in a serious, coaxing voice. "He's *very* concerned with stage presence." She paced the floor of the cabin called Oz with determined swing-steps, her knees locked like a soldier. She had a pencil in one ear and was wearing her reading glasses.

"Have you guys decided on three songs yet?" she continued. "Choice of music is equally as important as the performance itself."

The members of Bandit gathered around the cabin's stone fireplace. Jay Wong poked at a red ember log, trying to renew the flame; he listened to Zoe passively. I was beside Jay on the hearth. Abbey sat in a beat-up rocking chair; the chair creaked as she rocked it. Seth sat Indian style on an oval rug in front of the fireplace; charcoal-black holes made from flying sparks dotted the oval rug around Seth. Seth's earnest expression resembled Zoe's.

Seth took a sip of tea and honey and said, "I'm still for the two originals that we spoke of before, 'My National Anthem' and 'Evergreen Punk.'"

"Yeah," said Jay, "we gotta show we're inspired by Tahoe."

Abbey started to sing:

You stupid log
I axed you a mop better than peroxide
Could!
Shake it, so shake it.
Shake it, so shake it.

There's a termite
In your gut and I tried to
Cut it!
Shake it, so shake it.
Shake it, so shake it.

Evergreen Punk—
Cellulose nothin' 'cept for your
Hair!

Seth gestured for Abbey to be quiet. "We'll also need a copy tune, something contemporary, good for dancing. That new song by the Go-Gos is cool. We play that one tight." Seth's gray eyes roamed from person to person. "We've got to show the manager that Bandit has uniqueness."

"We could work a bass solo into the Go-Go tune," Jay offered. "I'll make the dude dig us. I'll make him think we're *bitchin'*." He laughed and tugged on a thin chain; the fireplace screen shut with a slipping metal noise.

"Be serious," Zoe told him.

Jay continued to be unserious and closed his eyes tightly, and furiously shook his head full of thick black hair, as if he were getting into some wild concert playing in his mind. After a while, his brown eyes blinked open, and he became motionless. "What's everyone looking at me for? I'm just trying to psych myself up."

"We're trying to make a decision about something," Abbey said.

"I thought we already had it figured out. The three tunes Seth's talking about are cool with me."

I gave a thumbs up, too. Abbey agreed with Seth.

She stood and said, "That was a good meeting. Thank you, Zoe. Wasn't that a good meeting, you guys?"

"Very corporate," I said.

Zoe hadn't been able to line up any work for us other than our steady but demeaning engagement at the Hofbrau. Seth grumbled about it and tried to get us work himself, and had no better luck than Zoe. Getting gigs in Tahoe was a lot tougher than in San Luis Obispo.

We took our places and played the three songs over and over. No one wanted to fail.

It was one of those times where we were able to use anxiety as a tool, let it fill us, then channel it into a creative force, which spurred Bandit to play without error—perfectly in the groove.

*   *   *

I didn't have much time to be nervous as I set up my drums onstage. I adjusted the spacing between the two cymbals on the hi-hat and snugged the wing nut; the ride and crash cymbals still weren't positioned quite right; I hoped there would be time to tune the head on my snare; the big room made it sound flat. Trickles of sweat rolled down my forehead.

"You guys about ready?" asked Case Johnson, the manager of the Lake Club. "Jesus, I have appointments today. You people think you're the only ones on my calendar?" He stood behind the bar eating green martini olives. He chewed them snappily, as if they were kernels of popcorn. Before he tossed an olive into his mouth, he speared the stuffed pimento with a toothpick and flicked it indignantly into the sink.

Case Johnson carried himself like an American tough-guy, his upper torso kept stiff, his butt tucked in. He wore a silk suit and men's jewelry made out of gold nuggets.

He snatched up another green martini olive and said, "Why can't they make these things without these goddamn red things? Jesus." His eyes traveled around the stage and stopped on Seth, who was taping down some loose mike cords with duct tape. Seth had a pet peeve about loose cords onstage. Seth thought loose cords were unprofessional.

"What the hell are you doing up there?" Case Johnson yelled. "This is just an audition. What the hell are you doing? We'll never get you people torn down in time for the Pronouns to get set up tonight. Jesus."

But Seth wouldn't stop taping for anyone, and—moving just a little quicker—he finished concealing the cords leading from the mike stands to the the P.A. mixer. Case Johnson flung another pimento into the sink behind the bar and strode out of the room.

Sly was on the stage with Seth, Jay, and me. "Is there anything I can do to help, gents?" she asked. Sly and Jay had been to the beach. Jay still had on his baggies and flip-flop sandals, and Sly was wearing a short, terrycloth jumpsuit over her bikini. Her tanned arms and legs shined from suntan oil. She looked sexy.

Jay replied, "Just take a seat, baby. The boys have it handled." Jay cracked me up when he was with his woman. He acted like they were a couple playing house. Jay Wong was in love.

Sly crossed her tanned legs and adjusted herself so that her swimming suit top didn't poke out. "Don't worry about Case," she said. "He's just got a bloody temper." She made a happy screwed-up face. "He's bloody fond of himself, too."

My drums were ready. I wondered where Abbey and Zoe were. I looked to the upper level, the promenade encased in chain-link fence. The girls weren't sitting on one of the terraces. My eyes continued around the club's interior, until they locked onto a gun-blue metal statue.

It was a one-dimensional man, cut from a flat sheet of

metal; the figure was welded upright onto a pedestal, an empty 50-gallon oil drum. Spherical droplets of frozen metal remained from the blowtorch. The man's edges were jagged and rough. Cut into the uppermost contour was a rectangular shape representing the head. Its only features were two eye holes, side-by-side and slightly staggered.

Now there are eyes, and then there are eyes. Witchy green eyes. Cat's eyes. X-ray eyes. Doll's eyes. Glass eyes that are mirrors. Eyes that are smart. Eyes that are sappy and stupid. The blowtorch man's eyes were vacant holes, air and nothing-ness eyes. These eyes were a negative exposure of an old-fash-ioned gun slinger's eyes. These eyes were spookily staring me down.

Abbey and Zoe entered through the back door to the private dock. Zoe peppered Abbey with words, "Oh my, my, my. That wasn't very smart. Are you going to be okay? Are you sure?"

Abbey skipped over to the stage, leaving Zoe behind. "Hi, you guys. Hi, Sly. Hi, Danny." Her voice sounded silly.

Zoe joined us and looked around for the manager. When she saw that Case Johnson wasn't around, Zoe said to Seth, "Abbey took a Quaalude. She's pretty high."

Seth threw his skinny arms into the air. "I can't believe this," he said. "Shit, this is great. Just great." He glared at Abbey.

Abbey looked like she was about to cry. She mumbled, "I's needed something to relax. Tiz okay. Really, Seth." She broke into laughs. "Hey, you gguuuuyyyys. So's what? Huh? So's what? Let's go, go, go. *I want to sing.*"

Case Johnson reappeared. "Jesus, this isn't some kind of ice cream social. Get up on the stage and let's hear what you people got. Okay, already?" He fixed himself a highball.

Jay raised his eyebrows and said, "Here goes nothing."

Seth and Zoe said nothing and refused to look at Abbey. Abbey looked at me and winked. I winked back, even though I, too, was very disappointed in her.

The sad thing of it was, she actually pulled herself together. She sang all of her parts okay—on key, without any slurring, and without mistakes. Technically, none of us made any mistakes at all.

But still, something was missing that day. The songs just didn't sound as good as they had when we practiced them at the cabin.

Case Johnson told us airily that it was no dice. He dismissed us, eager to get us out of the club so that "the real thing," the Pronouns, could set up for their show that night. No one said much as we packed up our equipment to go home. I wanted to get the hell out of there before "He," "She," "Us," "Them," and "It" showed up. Sly slipped away to change into her cocktail dress. "Maybe next time, gang," she told us.

Abbey offered Seth a cigarette, and Seth said nastily, "Do you think this makes up for it?" He got down on his knees with the cigarette dangling from his lips and tore up his duct tape. Making sure his voice was loud enough so that Abbey could hear him, Seth muttered, "Stage presence. That means acting like a professional."

Seeming quite sober, Abbey walked to the side of the stage and sat down on the stage floor in a heap. Soon, Zoe gave in and went to comfort her spiritual sister.

I found myself looking at the blowtorch man. I gazed into the two holes that represented his eyes and, once again, saw something where there was nothing. That friggin' statue had a message: Case Johnson had looked into Bandit's eyeholes searching for lines of flux of invisible *juice*—the creative spirit and unthrottled ambition that gives a young band (in addition to good musicianship) poise and presence onstage.

Case Johnson saw nothing in Bandit's eyeholes, because something had happened that threw the band's mood for a loop.

For the first time ever I was really pissed off at Abbey.

*   *   *

Eddy said he just got out of bed when Abbey, Jay, Sly, and I arrived at his place. He looked groggy and stoned from sleep, and his polo shirt was untucked and rumpled at the waistline of his trousers. Eddy's skin seemed to be covered with a visible stickiness. He smelled strong like yeast.

Eddy squinted and tried to push down a tuft of reddish hair that had been ironed backwards, but as soon as his hand left it, the hair popped up again. Outside, it was noon and a crystal-clear summer day in Tahoe.

"Please, come in," he said quietly. He examined Abbey and Sly in their short summer clothes. It was a little crude the way his eyes went between their legs. The girls didn't notice what he was doing, but Jay and I did. Jay laughed.

"This is a super house," Sly exclaimed. "You must be quite wealthy. You aren't in the market for a concubine, are you?" Sly put her arm around Jay's waist and squeezed to let Jay know she was just flirting.

"It's my parent's house," Eddy said. "However, you know what they say, dear girl. When the cat's away the mouse will play." Eddy was trying to act real suave.

"Such a nice gent you are," Sly said. "We'll all have to make ourselves right at home then."

"Indeed," said Eddy. "Please do." I kind of felt like telling Eddy to shut up.

Eddy directed Jay and me to the wet bar and told us to help ourselves. He invited the girls on a tour of the lake house. When Eddy wasn't looking, Sly indicated to Jay via a mocking expressing that she thought Eddy was full of shit, but continued to humor Eddy to his face. "A tour?" Sly said to the host. "That's a super idea."

I motioned for Abbey to go with Eddy. "This house is really amazing. Have a look." Abbey looked irritated. She was no cocktail waitress and wasn't used to dealing with rich Don Juans like Edward. She was used to the role of queen rather than saucy wench.

"This way, ladies. Your honorable tour guide is waiting with bated breath," Eddy said.

"God," Abbey said, "you're so sophisticated. I'm sssooo impressed."

"Hey, what can I say?" Eddy said. "What can I say?" Excitedly, he led the girls up the spiral staircase.

The house tour gave Jay and me a chance to relax and slug down some of Eddy's liquor. When Abbey returned, I wasn't going to let her out of my sight for the rest of the day. It was time for her and me to have a little fun. After we blew it at the Lake Club audition, the spirit of Bandit sank low. Zoe quickly forgave Abbey. The two spiritual sisters stuck together like glue and acted bitchy and exclusive. Seth snarled at everyone. Jay and I maintained low profiles. Then, Zoe came through with a new gig at the Lone Star nightclub, a respectable place. We told Mickey and his Hofbrau to take a hike. The sonofabitch owed us $500.

Eddy returned with the girls. "Have you seen his boat?" Abbey asked me.

"It's pretty nice, isn't it," I said.

"Eddy says later he'll take us out on the lake," she said. She put her lips to my ear. "That should be more exciting than his stupid little tour."

Sly put her hand on Abbey's shoulder. "Us girls are having a super time. Aren't we, Abbey?"

"If you say so," she said, "then I guess I am." Her smile was incredibly fake.

Abbey was a funny bird. Onstage she was so dynamic and open, yet offstage she made it difficult for people to be her friend. She came off as being a stuck-up bitch. To me, it seemed, Abbey just didn't trust people.

Eddy brought out a plastic zip-lock baggie filled with dried brown and black mushrooms. "Look at those puppies," Jay said. "Thirty bucks, right? Man, I haven't 'shroomed in ages." Talk of money was just a courtesy. Eddy always gave Bandit drugs for free. Jay opened the bag and took one of the mushrooms and held it to his nose.

"Here, check it out, man." Jay handed the fungus umbrella to me. The stem and the head, with dark paper ribs underneath, were covered with a dry powder, though the mushroom was resilient and bendable.

"You eat these things?" I said. "They smell like dirt."

Now that the drugs were on the table, we had a common denominator. The dope made everyone best friends. Sly held a mushroom under Abbey's nose. Sly's gesture was careful and feminine.

"Nice," Abbey said. "I can't wait." Abbey looked at Sly and Sly looked at Abbey and the girls seemed to share a newfound secret.

Dope bent people. Even the prospect of doing dope bent people. Sly became Zoe. Eddy became one of us instead of a groupie dealer. Did Bandit bend us, too? In Abbey's mind was I a substitute?

I ate four mushrooms. They tasted like they smelled and went down like vitamins.

M   M   M

12:30 P.M. It's been over a half hour and I feel nothing and think that these 'shrooms—as Jay and everyone else calls them—are dud firecrackers. Still, I am nervous. I wonder if I am going to die.

We are all good friends now, and Eddy plays his stereo for us and I drum on the coffee table because I am nervous and don't know what's going to happen. I wonder if I will hallucinate. Or freak out. I remember all the movies I saw in the early seventies when I was in junior high school. There was a big drug scare in the schools then. We watched movies in our humanities classes about kids who thought they had snakes crawling all over them. The films tried to show all the colors and distortion that the kids saw. The films read like a comic strip. One kid in the films got high and blew his head off with a twelve-gauge shotgun. He only wanted to kill the snakes that were crawling all over him.

I am confident the films were propaganda because alcohol, grass, cocaine, and uppers just seem to turn down reality and make you happy. If you take too much, you don't get the snakes—you throw up. I feel smug. I figure mushrooms will be sort of the same.

The new drug begins to take effect. I tell Abbey it feels just like I'm getting drunk. She hugs me and tells me to wait. I wait. I notice that Eddy's house is very tidy. I wonder if he or his sister cleans it. Thinking of Tish makes me nervous and also turns me on. I want to make it with Abbey. I think that while we're on 'shrooms she'll finally let me. I am turned on and tingling.

1:10 P.M. I keep looking at my watch like this is an experiment. We leave in the Blue Max. *It is warm outside. I take off my shirt and drink the sun. Abbey and I sit in the bow. She acts like she is sharing this thing with me. Like she knows what's in my mind and I know what's in her mind. I put my arms around her. I am still turned on, but not as much. I want her to take her top off and get a tan, but she says she is not wearing a bathing suit.*

I touch her legs with my legs. The boat bounces with powerful lunges in the water. Eddy lets Jay drive. Dope bends. The high is different than my past experiences. This is a trip. I am tripping. I am glad there are no snakes. The water is bluer but still water. The boat is bigger but still a boat. The mountain caps high above the lake are like a painting. The sky and the fact that it keeps going out into space seems more important than the mountains. But the sky is the sky and the mountains are the mountains.

We stop and float. Eddy and Jay smoke a joint. I think they are crazy. I am very drugged already. I hope they don't die. I kiss Abbey. I start to notice that I am this human with two parts—this essence that is thinking right now, and the body that this essence is stuffed into. I make the essence float up and hover above my body. I try to make the essence fly up onto the mountain tops, but it is chained to my body with a leash. The leash is about four or five feet long. I realize that the body wants Abbey and that my essence doesn't give a damn. I realize that most of the time this essence tricks me and makes me think I'm just one thing, not two. I want the separation to stop. Now. But I remain split. I tell Abbey that I want the mushrooms to wear off. She smiles and says, "Enjoy them. They last a long time." I am scared even without the snakes.

2:49 P.M. My watch is talking to me. It sounds like an insect. I want this stuff to wear off. Time moves slowly. I have to pay my dues.

Eddy is really fucked up. So is Jay. They are drinking and smoking joints. Abbey and Sly keep laughing. Everything is funny to the girls. They all ask me why I am so quiet. This is fun they say. It is a trip they say. They swim and dive off the boat. I am worried the boat will start and cut somebody up. They keep swimming near the prop.

Eddy slips and cracks his elbow on a metal cleat. He is bleeding. He has just come out of the lake and is wet. The blood stream mixes into the thin sheet of water on his freckled body. It is a bad cut. Sly says she can see the bone. She wraps his arm in a towel. Jay gets Eddy another beer. Eddy thinks hurting himself is a joke. "Ouch," he says. "I've got an ouchy, Mommy." Everyone starts laughing again. Jay howls, "Ouchy, ouchy, ouchy."

4:15 P.M. Eddy's lake house. Eddy wants to watch TV. He is tired from the boat ride and his arm is sore. We leave him and go away.

My essence keeps hovering over me. I am still split in two. I am a character in a movie. My essence is watching me. Abbey keeps touching me. I don't want anyone to touch me. I want to crawl inside myself. I think of the snakes.

Jay is really fucked up. He drives up a dirt fire road to the top of a mountain. He wants to see a view. We park. Abbey knows I'm *freaking out. She is being nice. She hovers over me. I tell her not to touch me. She says we need to walk. Jay and Sly stay behind. They are going to do it in the van. I know. My essence wants to watch them. My body is repulsed by the touching.*

I tell Abbey she is being nice, and tell her not to touch me because I am separated. We walk. It is starting to get dark and I see a woodpecker. The bird is pecking. Knock. Knock. Knock. I reach down and pick up some bark and give it to Abbey for payment for taking care of me. The forest smells like sap. I am not getting sober, but I am not getting any more head rushes now.

We walk back. Jay and Sly are playing frisbee in the dusk. They are not screwing. They are both athletes. Abbey talks to Jay and Sly. I pretend like I can't hear but I can, "He's getting better...it was so cute, he gave me a piece of bark...."

Jay slaps me on the shoulder and asks me if I had a good trip. I lie and say, "Yes."

"Bitchin'," he says.

7:00 P.M. We are buying groceries. Sly and Abbey are still girlfriends. They are going to make dinner at Sly's. I am not split anymore. But everything is still bent. Abbey and I hold hands in the store. Her hand feels okay. She is leading me around as if I were a child.

We will barbecue chicken. I enjoy the shopping. I enjoy looking at all the labels. Everywhere I look there is something interesting in the fine print: "$2.19/#, taste-O-fine!, Thiamine Mononitrate, push down and twist counter-clockwise to open child-proof cap, SALE ITEM, imported from Korea, artificial flavor, Yellow 5 color, Monosodium Glutamate, COUPON INSIDE BOX, contains partially hydrogenated soybean or palm oil...."

Abbey finds a package of chicken. There is a bright orange sticker on the cellophane that says, "Great on the grill." There is an old couple next to us. They are mountain people. His clothes are dirty. She has a big frayed hole in the back of her sweater. They are looking at chuck roasts. They are proud people. They stand up straight and proud and

*search through the packages until they find one they like. He finds a
small one but says it's old and brown. She finds a bigger one. She
seems delighted that they will buy the big one. We buy our groceries
and the mountain people are in front of us. They buy their food with
food stamps. The man buys a pack of cigars and some candy for his
wife with his own green money, a $5 bill.*

*The old mountain couple are so beautiful that I want to cry. I
feel the floor beneath my feet. I am heavy and my bare feet are pressed
against the flat, cool floor. I am off the 'shrooms. I am glad I didn't
die. I am glad I didn't see the snakes. I feel very lucky. I feel like a
loser.*

M M M

It was past midnight when Abbey and I got back to the
cabin called Oz. Jay stayed at Sly's apartment, and we drove
home in the van. It was peaceful in the cabin. Zoe and Seth
were deep in sleep. Upstairs, Seth's snoring was rhythmical and
low. This sound of sleep blended nicely with the dull whine of
the electric clock in the kitchen and the dark vacuous breeze of
the forest outside.

A big smoldering log in the fireplace cracked and popped as
sap boiled deep in its core. A wispy flame hung on top of the
chunk of firewood, the flame going *whoosh whoosh* trying to stay
alive. Aside from the firelight that seeped through the fireplace
screen, a vintage darkness seasoned the cabin; it was as if we
had disappeared inside a huge cask, the wooden walls aged and
stained from dark purple wine.

I stoked the fire, and the flame, which moments before
cowered with dying breaths, now voraciously engulfed the fresh,
dry log I threw on. Abbey and I lay in front of the hearth on fat
pillows that smelled of mold and the pickling forest scent. We
entwined ourselves like stacked spoons—her front to the fire
and her back pressing against the front of me. We lay very still
and watched the fire move.

Abbey's voice was a quiet saxophone. "You scared me today. All that stuff you kept saying. Being split. Being separated." As she talked into the fire, her words bounced off the flames and flew back like little spirits. "How come that weird stuff never happens to me?"

"I don't know," I answered. "Drugs affect different people differently, I guess. In you, drugs play like music. In me, sometimes they play like—, like a charade. Sometimes the mask they make me wear doesn't fit so well. The mask digs in." I placed my hand on the slope of Abbey's hip and gently gripped it, feeling underneath my fingers the sleek bone darting toward her pelvis. I withdrew my caress and said, "Eddy's the one that really cracks me up. Drugs make him think he's Superman. He's the kind that's going to kill himself on them."

"Who cares about Eddy?" Abbey said. She took my tentative hand and clasped it tightly against her bosom. I felt Abbey's fingers drawing imaginary pictures on my palm. She was sending signals of affection that she had never sent before, and I was both delighted and frozen.

My eyes rode her curves like a roller coaster. Her faded jeans, her girly stockings with snowflakes stitched on them, her silky blouse untucked at the waistline, her wonderful herbal smell.

Gingerly, I stroked the tip of one of her breasts through her blouse and camisole. I touched her so faintly that I wasn't sure if she noticed. My perception narrowed until I heard nothing but our breathing and the crackle of the fire. The moment was so pleasurable it made me dizzy. I wondered if I was separating again.

Abbey said, "That feels nice." Beneath my fingers I felt a hard knot, and I cupped the breast with newfound boldness. While my fingers played, Abbey hummed quietly, the way people do when they dream, in low chirps and singing exhales. The thought of making love to Abbey made my heart do pirouettes inside my chest.

She rolled on her back and smiled at me. Her green eyes were full of glassy orange diamonds from the fire, and her brown hair flowed sexily all over the faded pillow. "It's time," she said. "I think we're both ready."

"Thanks," I said.

"Thanks for what? We haven't done anything yet," she said. Coy and sweet and sassy—that was Abbey Butler.

I slipped my hand under her top and felt her hidden flesh. I moved on top of her and kissed her passionately. I became afraid when she pushed me away.

Her eyes were full of orange diamonds again. "We better go upstairs," she said. I took her hand.

I lit a candle and apologized for the rumpled underwear that was strewn on the crates Jay and I had made into a dresser. The loft was a meager and simple space underneath slanted, unfinished rafters; in places, toothpicks of silver night peeked through the lattice of shingles. But it was my turf, my element. I felt increasingly bold and sensual there with Abbey.

We stood and began our lovemaking systematically. I unbuttoned her blouse and tossed it on Jay's bunk. She kissed me hotly and pulled off my T-shirt. It got stuck around my neck because she was too careful; so I intervened and ripped it off. My face stung as she claimed her prize and threw it side-armed onto Jay's bunk.

The pace quickened, and my hands moved all over her. From her charming face that was still candy-red from the sunshine, to the languid curves of her churning and wiggling slim buttocks, to her soft naked breasts and perfect nipples, erect from both delight and the chilly mountain air.

Her hands moved all over me, too, responding and inquiring.

Deep kisses. We siphoned each other's spirits back and forth, back and forth, as though we were mixing our passion in two swirling glasses of brandy.

I got on my knees to remove the chastity of Abbey's final garment. I was already naked and openly stiff. Her panties were tiny and of the same dull white silk as her camisole. Above the hidden fluff between her legs was a dainty bow sewn onto the middle of the elastic band. I nuzzled her. Her hips danced a slow waltz. She hummed more loudly a melody of sleepy love sounds.

I removed her panties so that we could finally come together. The nakedness between her legs was more womanly than I had imagined—thicker and more symmetrical. In the crease of one leg, between her pelvis and upper thigh where the elastic of her panties still left an impression, was a small mole the size of a grain of coarse pepper. The dark spot was moving and beautiful.

We lay on my bed and continued to breathe each other's breaths, our darting tongues mimicking the motion that was beginning between our bodies. Abbey's humming exhales turned to passionate moans, and she spread her legs to share herself. I let my face travel to her smooth, flat belly and kissed it and felt tantalizing heat steaming inches below. I arched forward, and our bodies slipped together with a perfect fit.

Chapter 9
Mr. Clobber's Wild Ride

Love mends, and, like dope, love bends....

"It's hard to believe it's already August," I said. Jay and I were sitting on Schooner Pier, our favorite hangout on the lake front. There was a nip to the morning air, and I wished I had brought along a sweatshirt or something.

We hoped Eddy would stay true to his word and take us out for a pull that morning. Both Jay and I watched the horizon for the *Blue Max*. Yet we knew not to become overzealous. Eddy was flaky—sometimes he showed up when he said he would, and sometimes he didn't.

"Look at the lake, just a slight chop," Jay said, "—fucking primo, dude. I'll bet over in Emerald Bay it's as smooth as glass." He raised his eyebrows. "If that donkey, Eddy, shows, I'm going to give you some water ski lessons today. I'm going to show you how to *shred*." He gave me a hearty slap on the back. I felt warmer.

"What's Sly up to? Isn't it her day off?" I asked.

Jay shrugged his sinewy shoulders. "Yeah, she's going shopping with Abbey and Zoe." His face looked uneasy, like a parent's face looks when his kid does something new on his own. "They called her up last night, said they're going to South Shore."

"I think it's good that the girls are all getting along."

"It's cool, I guess," Jay said. "I'm going to see Sly tonight." He grinned and exposed the silver caps on his eyeteeth. "I have some major sperm build-up I need taking care of, dude. I'm going to give my lady an extra large hot beef injection."

Jay and I both laughed devilishly.

Seriously, I did think it was nice that the girls were getting together with Sly. Other than the one time we did 'shrooms, Abbey acted icy toward her. In fact, when Abbey and I were alone, sometimes she made fun of Sly: "That accent of hers is probably a fake. She just wants you guys to think she's chic. God, and the way she bounces around and sticks her boobs out...."

I couldn't find anything wrong with Sly, myself. She treated Jay like a king. I wished Abbey was as openly affectionate with me.

Abbey Butler's relationship with me was tenuous. It had a way of wringing me out like a wet dishrag. Abbey didn't have a big heart. She had, I decided, a high-quality small heart, which could issue affection so pure and so strong that it was addictive. She could also shut it off in an instant.

Jay finished cleaning the lenses of his Vuarnet sunglasses and retied the bandana around his neck, then put his shades back on with cool precision.

"Do you love Sly?" I asked.

Jay leaned over the edge of the pier and hurled a scoopful of icy water onto me.

I felt cold again.

"Hey, wait a minute. Is that Eddy?" He pointed at a blue ski boat that, from our perspective on the pier, was only about an inch long. We watched the boat's image grow as it moved toward Schooner Pier at an angle.

The boat turned sharply, whipped a skier in a graceful arc, and then headed away. It wasn't the *Blue Max*.

"Shit," Jay said. He lay down on the faded wood pier and told me to keep watch.

I stared at the lake for a long while. Its surface captured the crisp, morning-time beauty like a painting. Brush-strokes of purple, green, and gray whisked over the blue canvas; ripples made curved mirrors to wink back at the sun. The thing about Lake Tahoe was that it was so gut-wrenchingly vivid, sometimes it frightened me.

"Why's she such a fuck-up?"

Jay didn't answer.

"I'm talking about Abbey."

He sat up and carefully surveyed the lake for Eddy. "She's a rock 'n' roller. Being a party hound comes with the job. Lighten up, donkey."

"It pisses me off how she wipes herself out sometimes," I continued. "Like at the Lake Club audition. Why did she freak out and rip reality out of the ground? What do you suppose she's keeping from us, when she escapes into Never-Never Land?"

"Look it," Jay said. "You party, I party. You have secrets, I have secrets. Not many chicks are like Abbey. Not many chicks can sing like Abbey. She's no angel. The reality of it is, man— she never will be."

Jay's smug, cool attitude was chafing on me.

Neither he nor the rest of the members of Bandit said much about it, but everyone knew he was coming. There were flyers all over the place. The friggin' *Tahoe Tribune* ran a half-page ad in the entertainment section.

"What the hell is going to happen when the Pricey Dexters show up for their Labor Day gig?" I asked. "I have a feeling their drummer is going to be a pain-in-the-ass."

"I'm looking forward to seeing him, myself," said Jay. "I like the dude. So I'm asking you to give him some respect."

"Sorry," I said.

"It's about you and Abbey, I know," he said. "But I was there, dude. Dom and Abbey ended up hating each other's guts. I don't know what the whole story was. But listen to this, when Abbey split that was it with her and my buddy, Dom. I've known her for longer than you have, dude. She likes you. She cares for you."

There was something in Jay's speech, however, that didn't underscore what he said. It was the cadence of his voice, the way he tried to rush through the facts and get the topic over with.

We waited until one o'clock, and Eddy finally showed. It had gotten choppy on the lake, and few skiers were out on the water. Jay and I didn't give a damn. We went for it and beat our legs to death, out on the big, blue lake.

*　　*　　*

The only western prop left in the Lone Star was a mechanical bull named "Mr. Clobber." When the bar used to be an Okie club, the bull was named "Thunder 'n' Lightning," and some people, like Mike, the bartender, still referred to it that way.

The bull's new name was associated with skiing, Tahoe's *numero uno* sport. The verb "to clobber" is local dialect meaning "to crash" or "to wipe-out."

Tacked onto the wall in the back room where we dressed, there were some snapshot photos of the Lone Star *Version One*. Sawdust on the floor. Checkered tablecloths. Cocktail waitresses dressed like cowgirls. Mike, the bartender, dressed like an Indian. In front there even used to be a sign of a cowhand roping a lone star with a lariat. Now, there was a sign of a skier doing a back-scratcher, with a lone neon star plunked over his head.

The Lone Star *Version Two* was your basic post-disco era, jogger generation, class "A" nightclub, and I endorsed all renovations made except one. The bull I saw in the snapshots had dignity—he was a thoroughbred creature. "Thunder 'n' Lightning" was sleek. His saddle looked oiled, his metal unrusted, and his two glass eyes had a proud, noble glint.

Now he was very ill kept.

His hide was miserable and ragged; his saddle was worn and cracked; his metal was tarnished; and his right eye was missing and now just a frayed socket. Somebody placed a ski hat—the elfy, pointed kind with a little fluff ball on top—on poor Clobber's crown. Nailed to the underside of his rear quarters were two stuffed socks. When they jiggled everyone would laugh.

Something else about Mr. Clobber was that his control lever was "ca-broke." The settings in the middle didn't work, leaving only two extremes—low and high. Because of his faulty circuitry, he bucked and spun in only one direction.

Mr. Clobber's repertoire was like night and day. On "low," the bull spun and rocked gaily like a merry-go-round. On "low," one imagined the toots of a pipe organ. On "high," one imagined the *rup-rup-rup* of a jackhammer. On "high," the bull erupted like a volcano and broke arms and legs, squashed nuts (and a few ovaries), and created outrageous bar tabs. The latter consequence was why the owner kept the bull around.

Since we'd started playing there, Bandit had started a tradition at the Lone Star. Every night at twelve midnight we quit playing for a half hour and Abbey emceed a rodeo. Jay and I normally took a whirl on the bull ourselves. Seth was chicken. Zoe was too smart for such nonsense. Abbey, thank God, enjoyed conducting her rodeo so much that she didn't get on the bull—just threatened to.

That night, the first rider was a female customer. There were a couple of gals who were pro snow skiers, and they could give any guy in the place a run for his money. These daring ladies requested the high setting and rode Mr. Clobber as easily as they negotiated six-foot moguls on the expert slopes of Squaw Valley. They were human, though. The week before, a stocky little brunette "got clobbered"; and, after she mopped herself up, she kicked the poor bull right in the friggin' socks.

The manager had to nail Mr. Clobber's woolen anatomy back on—right then and there—to pacify the crowd.

The first contestant of the evening, a buxom girl—who was not a pro skier—mounted Mr. Clobber and requested the low setting, and that meant the bull's reputation was in jeopardy. Abbey made everyone in her rodeo wear a ceremonial cowboy hat. Rider #1 put on the beat-up straw hat that was so big it covered her ears, and proceeded to slowly spin and rock. After guzzling a flaming shot for the crowd and symbolically licking the shot glass, the buxom girl started making rude S-shaped motions on the bull that drew catcalls and copious cheers.

Moo!

Abbey Butler liked a spectacle. But sometimes she was known to side with the bull. Her mischievous grin whetted the crowd's appetite, and an anxious rumble filled the Lone Star.

"Well now," she announced, managing a sort of western accent. "I think this little rodeo queen deserves some excitement." She cued the band, and we played a scratchy riff in F minor that started very slow, and then got faster and faster and faster. Abbey yelled, "Hit it, Mike," and the bartender who ran Clobber's switch slipped the lever from "low" to "high." A prouder Mr. Clobber bucked rider #1 on her pert little ass, to the cheers of all.

Jay grabbed his woodgrain Fender Precision bass—the neck with his left hand and the body with his right—and in a swift, fluid motion ducked under the shoulder strap. He placed the instrument on its stand. "Let's go for it."

"After you," I said. I gave him a shove toward Abbey, with her ceremonial cowboy hat.

Jay went the designated two minutes on high without a moment where his balance was in question. He also wowed the crowd with his latest trick, which was to jump to a standing position and act like he was surfing, negotiating the bucks of Mr. Clobber like mounds of tumbling Pacific.

My turn.

When Mr. Clobber was cranked up, just to hang on in a sitting position took agility and concentration. The key was to not fight it, to get in sync with the *rup-rup-rup*, the whirl of forces.

A rider and bull have a similar relationship to a drummer and bassist. A drummer provides the back beat and, in a sense, presides over a band's rhythm like a rider presides over an animal. At the same time, a good drummer tailors the beat to the bass line so that the product is two complementary sounds pulsing in unison. The drummer leads the bassist; the bassist leads the drummer. Especially in a jam session where the band makes up the song as they play it, good rhythm is a matter of having a sixth sense. Drummers have to be mind-readers; robotic bull riders have to predict the beast's crazy motion, or else bust their balls and get thrown on their faces.

Other nights, when I had tried to stand, I failed to maintain a firm slip-grip on the rope halter as I let out the slack. I noticed that when Jay went to the standing position, he kept himself stable by leaning back against a taut halter, keeping tension on it while sliding his grip. Steadily and fluidly, he swung to standing, the technique similar to a rock climber's rappel.

This time, to my excitement, I was able to keep tension on the halter. I found myself standing, knees soft, leg muscles tense. The sensation was thrilling and frightening as I loomed from side to side, feeling like a nervous driver oversteering a car. Not with the grace and style of Jay Wong, but with unembellished determination, I rode out minute number two.

I threw Abbey the cowboy hat, feeling like a hero. It made me feel good that she looked proud.

"Right on, dude."

Jay and I chinked beer mugs. I drained my glass.

"This place is bitchin'," he said. "Man, I could hang out

here forever. Fuck money. Fuck security. Fuck politics and Uncle Sam. Fuck the future. Fuck getting a new surfboard. Man, give me that bull anytime. Right now I'm thinking that bull is the most bitchin' thing in the world." He let out a howl. A chorus of wild, excited cheers filled the club. Mr. Clobber and bull riders, it seemed, filled the Lone Star with *juice*.

For some reason that night I didn't get the *juice*. I howled, too. But my loud noise sounded embarrassing, made me uneasy.

I had just ridden the bull, rode that friggin' thing standing, just like I had wanted. But what I had done seemed stupid.

I was thinking of my father, with his "level-head." I was seeing the nightclub through his eyes. The goings-on in the Lone Star were ludicrous, absurd.

Heavy thoughts. Did it mean anything at all to ride a mechanical bull? Did sheer fun justify fun?

I went and got stoned and drunk. You live, then you die, I rationalized. There's no one correct recipe for what goes in between. What the hell if I'd decided to take the flavor. What the hell if I'd decided to infuse myself with *juice*, when I could get it. This was the consolation prize, I rationalized, the consolation prize for a loser.

*   *   *

Seth pierced the cellophane and let his thumbnail glide between the edges of thin sheets of cardboard, corner to corner, making a full-length slit in the brand-new record jacket. On front, the album cover displayed an artist's rendition of a foliage-covered brick wall with four painted figures dressed in preppie suits standing in front of it. One guy wore a striped necktie as a headband and had drumsticks sticking out of his front pocket. This guy, of course, was Domino.

Seth unsleeved the thin, groovy disc, and held it gingerly by its outside edge. He put Side A of *Ivy League Dropouts* by the Pricey Dexters on the turntable in the cabin called Oz.

The first cut played. "I have to admit, I like this. I wonder if every song is going to be as good?" Seth was wearing a pair of Zoe's overalls because he had neglected to do his laundry. As he bent down to pick up a burning cigarette balanced on an empty Coke can on the fireplace hearth, you could see a fuzzy panda bear sewn onto the back pocket of the overalls.

"Are you wearing Zoe's undies, too, dude?" said Jay.

Zoe blushed and stuck her tongue out at Jay. Seth stood holding his cigarette and shook his head.

"Jay's right," I told Seth, "you look like a friggin' closet queen." I was pissed at him for buying the Pricey Dexter's album.

"Come on, you guys," Abbey said. "I'm trying to listen to the record."

"Listen and learn," Zoe advised.

"Someday, this is supposed to be us," Abbey continued. "Someday, it would be nice if Bandit cut an album, too."

Seth, Jay, and the girls listened to the Pricey Dexters intently. I resigned to do the same. The album was pretty damn good, but that wasn't the point, and saying that the P.D.s were an inspiration for Bandit wasn't the point, either.

None of the others could hide it from me. Having this album playing in our cabin was like them having someone to dinner whom they'd disowned—it was an experiment, a test. They were peeking at him and his L.A. band through a knot hole and deciding whether or not they were going to unlatch the door and let him back into their favor. Labor Day weekend was just around the corner. And each member of Bandit had to decide what he or she was going to do when Domino and the Pricey Dexters arrived in Tahoe.

*   *   *

I thought taking the girls someplace, hauling them around, would feel like old times, but it didn't. On the way to the casinos, Abbey and Zoe didn't evade me with feline smiles, private jokes, or girlish half-telepathic conversation; rather, they each took turns talking to me individually. Abbey and I discussed our passion for seedy, glitzy cocktail shows. Zoe told me about how she wanted to learn craps. When she discovered I didn't know a damn thing about craps, she turned the conversation back over to Abbey and reclaimed her soft-cover copy of *Win, Win, Win: A Primer for Games of Chance* and flipped through pages. Dusk fell as we passed Meeks Bay, and when it became too dark for Zoe to read, she put the book into her briefcase.

My eyes stared straight ahead. After Meeks Bay, the road to South Shore became windy and treacherous—a ribbon of pavement cut in the mountains like an altitudinous crack.

"Learn anything?" I asked.

"I think I've gotten the gist of it," Zoe said.

The windy mountain road gave me white knuckles. It didn't seem to bother Zoe at all.

"Oh my, I think we all ought to try it. It's simple. Each shooter begins with a come-out roll. Seven or 11 he wins; 2, 3, or 12 he loses, 'craps out'; 4, 5, 6, 8, 9, and 10 combinations the shooter rolls until his point reappears, or—"

"Fascinating," I said.

"It sounds like an awfully fussy game," Abbey said. "I'm sure I wouldn't enjoy it. You might be good at it, Danny." She put her head on my shoulder and shut her eyes.

Zoe continued, "Play the pass line. Play the don't-pass line. Eight the hard way. According to this book, the main thing is you just have to know when to quit."

"Win or lose," I said.

"Shit," said Abbey.

"Win or lose," Zoe said.

She went on to discuss craps from a statistical point of view. Abbey groaned periodically. I punctuated Zoe's key points with words like "okay," "yes," "sure," and "ahum."

Over the course of the summer, Zoe had evolved into a new person. She had always been smart, but now she seemed to showcase her intelligence, wield it like weapon. She had developed into the type of person my father longed for me to be.

I didn't begrudge her for it—not much anyway. The new Zoe was an awesome manager. The Lone Star gig was netting Bandit excellent wages. What's more, Zoe was growing confident that she could get us another shot at the Lake Club. She was literally hounding Case Johnson to give us another chance.

She had a slick way of bossing us around without coming off the wrong way. She pushed Seth hard to write and expand our repertoire of original music. She wanted us to stop playing copy tunes, to play our own material exclusively. It had been a real trip to watch Zoe change from a sedate, brainy groupie into a dynamic businesswoman who carried a cordovan briefcase and wore a panama hat.

*　　*　　*

Standing in the lobby of Caesars Tahoe, Abbey said, "Look at all the people playing slots. They all have such funny expressions. My God, it's like they're hypnotized and seeing pink elephants."

"They're seeing bananas, cherries, and oranges," said Zoe.

Abbey pointed toward a middle-aged man wearing yellow trousers and a white shirt; he stood rigidly and fed three machines at once from a paper bucket full of quarters. "He's utterly tranquilized."

"Like a zombie," said Zoe. "Oh my."

The girls laughed. Abbey stepped on my toe with the heel of her most recently acquired boots—a semi-used pair of white cowgirl boots with leather fringe and silver studs—purchased at

Tahoe Thrift. "Come on," she said. "We're off to see the wizard."

We set forth toward the gaming tables like Dorothy, the Scarecrow, and the Cowardly Lion, and drew lugubrious looks from a few idle slot machine players, who had lost all of their nickels, dimes, and quarters. The rest of the gamblers didn't seem to notice us.

We found three open seats at a $2 ante blackjack table. Abbey patted the stool next to her, offering it to Zoe. "I see a twenty-five cent craps table over there. I guess I'll catch up with you two later."

"Stay with us and play twenty-one," Abbey coaxed.

"I have my heart set on playing craps. Besides, three's a crowd." Zoe's voice was full of the same sensibility it carried when she was conducting herself as Bandit's manager. Her decision was not to be contended. "Adieu," she said. "Meet you for the show."

"Are you sure?" Abbey called after her.

"I'm positively sure," she said, not looking back.

"Isn't she a sweetheart?" Abbey said. "She has it so together lately."

"You're sweeter," I said.

"You never quit, do you?" she said.

The cocktail show we planned on seeing later was a smoke 'n' fire pop song review, featuring a band from New York called Jo Tokyo. It was in the Coral Room, one of Caesar's two-drink minimum lounges.

Abbey didn't have any money at all after buying her new boots. So I gave the dealer a twenty and got back ten two-dollar chips. I gave half of them to Abbey. I figured if we bet the minimum and had a little luck, we could last long enough for one or two free drinks.

After playing a couple of hands, Abbey turned sideways and said, "I wish Zoe would find someone."

"Pay attention to the game," I said. "We don't have very much money."

Why did I keep getting such lousy cards? I held four low cards totaling fifteen, no aces. The dealer hit me with a jack, and I busted.

Abbey went bust, too. "Are you listening to me, Danny?"

"She's too busy planning Bandit's rise to fame to be interested in men," I said. My voice was quick and hyped by the cards.

Abbey motioned for the dealer to hit her new hand—once, twice. She folded. "Oh craps," she said. She was out of chips; so she took one from my pile, leaving me with only one chip myself. "Zoe's old-fashioned when it comes to men."

"Yeah, right," I said, not looking at Abbey but rather at the dealer's face, trying to get some kind of clue as to what he was holding.

I won my hand; Abbey won hers also. Now we each had four dollars.

"Men are such jerks," she said.

"What are you talking about?"

"Zoe," she said, putting her lips close to my ear. "She's still a virgin."

"Oh my," I said.

"Jerk," she said, "I wish I was, too."

We quit talking and played blackjack with cranky concentration. Why in the hell was Abbey suddenly so preoccupied with Zoe's love life? Why couldn't Abbey worry about our relationship instead of spending her thoughts on matchmaking for someone else? Even though I'd gotten close to her, there was a part of me that knew damn well she could cut me out of her life in an instant, and never bat her witchy green eyes.

The blackjack cards became friendly. Soon I was up ten dollars and Abbey looked like she was up about fifteen. The waitress brought a round of free drinks. Abbey held her rum and coke next to my gin and tonic for a toast.

"Fuckin' cheers," she said.

"To us," I said.

We both doubled our bets the next hand, and the dealer showed a blackjack. Easy come, easy go.

A few minutes later, Zoe reappeared. "You two are not going to believe who's here."

"Who?" I asked.

"A movie star?" Abbey said. "Someone famous?"

"I wish," Zoe said.

"Do we have to guess," I said, "or are you going to tell us?"

"I bet it's someone famous," Abbey said. "Is it David Bowie or Sting or someone like that?"

Zoe took off her panama hat and shook her short blonde hair as though her hair felt hot and was a nuisance. "No. *He's* here. I'm talking about Uwe."

"Shit," Abbey said. She took a cigarette out of her purse, lit it, and blew smoke through her nose.

"What on earth is Uwe doing here?" I asked.

"He's working at Caesars—" Zoe said, "in the casinos. I talked with him."

"I'm sure," Abbey said incredulously, "college graduates are just dying to get jobs in a casino in Lake Tahoe. Just watch. He's going to kiss up to us and try to get back in the band. That snake. Just watch."

"Seth was right," I said. "He did see Uwe cruise by the Hofbrau...spying on us."

"It's not that way. Hold on, you guys. Uwe told me he's applying to law school at Oakley Hindale. Not this fall, but the next one. He's taking a year off to make some money, ski, and that sort of thing. One of his fraternity brothers has a place in Heavenly."

"This whole thing is a pretty big coincidence," I said.

"Even though I still dislike him," Zoe said. "I think he told me the truth. He's too stupid to come up with such an outrageous scheme just to be around Bandit."

"That's a thought," Abbey said.

"Hindale is a very poor school," Zoe said. "I've heard that people buy their degrees there. I'm not sure if it's accredited. Plus, who would want to go to school in Sacramento?"

"I wouldn't," said Abbey.

"If we see him, are you going to be mean to him?"

"Yes."

"Good," Zoe said, "just so I know."

*   *   *

"Well if it isn't my comrades from Bandit," Uwe said. He was ushering for the ten o'clock show in the Coral Room.

Uwe had lost some weight and had a dark tan. He didn't have any zits on his face at all. He looked the best I had ever seen him.

"Hello, Uwe," said Abbey. "But whatever happened to your big job in L.A.? And all the bands Domino was going to get you in?"

"That piss-ant company reneged because 'technically' I don't have my degree yet. One of my bozo poly-sci profs gave me a 'D' spring quarter.

"It's no big deal. Hindale Law School will let me make it up."

"You've done the world a great service by giving up your keyboards," said Abbey.

He issued a superior smile. "Becoming a lawyer is what poly-sci majors do, Abbey-dearest, when they decide they want to make a whole bunch more money than piss-ant musicians."

We were holding up the line of people to be seated.

Uwe motioned for us to follow him. As he led us through the tables holding a flashlight, he said, "The way it works is that you people are supposed to give me a tip if you want a table up front. But forget it. I'm going to get you a great seat for nothing."

"Thanks," I said.

"Get me some tickets to one of your shows sometime," he said. "I like comedy acts. Just kidding, of course."

Uwe pointed to an excellent table—first row, front and center. The girls rushed ahead and claimed their seats, while Uwe and I followed behind them through the tight arrangement of tables. Still exhibiting his new polished manner and tone of voice, the old Uwe spoke from within— clandestinely, so no one could hear but me. "That sweet bitch, Abbey, still looks as sexy as ever. Zoe's looking pretty good these days, too. What do you say, Danny. Which one's spreading her legs for you? Or is it both, you sly dog."

"Have some respect, you friggin' donkey." I felt like slugging him in the face.

"No problem," he said, "just trying to make conversation. Just trying to keep up with old friends."

I took my seat. Uwe maintained his charade with the girls. "Will this table be all right, ladies?"

"It's gorgeous," Zoe said. Abbey looked to the stage, and forced herself to say thanks almost pleasantly.

Zoe shoved a couple bucks toward Uwe. He fanned away the tip. "I wouldn't think of it," he said. "Enjoy the show. Jo Tokyo is an excellent band. Of course, I can't even begin to compare them with Bandit."

He left to seat more customers. His presence lingered like the whining hum of an electric clock.

Chapter 10
Domino

"Abbey, I'm nervous. I'm nervous about us," I said, as I watched her finish dressing in front of a frameless mirror in her and Zoe's bedroom. The cabin's owner hadn't gotten around to putting up wallboard in this dim, windowless, little room. The walls were a negative exposure of pipes, electrical conduit, and skeletal two-by-fours. In the nooks and crannies, Abbey and Zoe had placed pinecones, candles from Izy's shop, and colorful rocks polished smooth by the lake. There were two mattresses lying along opposite walls, each covered with pillows and a thick quilt. On the cement floor between the beds was a fiesta-colored oval rug that Abbey told me she bought one time she and her mother took a train to Mexico. Directly in front of Abbey, on top of a pine dresser below the mirror, were myriad feminine potions, perfumes, and lotions, glinting blue and pink in glass vials.

"Having him over wasn't my idea," she said hurriedly. Bending over the dresser on her tiptoes, Abbey cocked her head to the right and looked sideways at her made-up profile, then examined the left side similarly. Satisfied, she touched up her nails and held her hands out like half-extended wings, fluttering her fingers impatiently to speed the drying process.

"Why on earth did Seth have to invite him?" I asked. "We're going to watch their show Sunday night. Good God, why can't Seth just wait and see him then?"

"Are you forgetting, he *did* used to play with us. And he told Seth he really wanted to visit. Domino is so gregarious. That's what Zoe says." Protective of her nails, Abbey pulled on a pair of tight jeans using only her thumbs, and wiggled her feet into a pair of short, maroon-colored boots with metal toe plates and spike heels. She checked her appearance a final time in the mirror. The fidgety anxiety her expression always took when she dressed and did her makeup was gone.

I was lying on her bed among purple and green silk pillows. She came and sat on the mattress edge.

"How do I look?"

"Nice."

"Are you sure?"

"Absolutely."

"Why are you so paranoid?" Her voice strove to be patient, but her eyes clearly showed disenchantment.

"Why can't you admit it? There's still something going on between you and Domino, isn't there?"

"You're acting kind of selfish, Danny. I want to get this whole Pricey Dexter thing over with, too. I'd much rather worry about Bandit's show, and *our* thing."

"Trying to talk with you about him is fruitless," I said. "Honestly, it's about as worthwhile as asking a friggin' zoo rhinoceros to explain why the function 'e raised to the power x' sends a curved line to infinity!"

"Talk some more math to me, Danny. It turns me on."

"Wicked."

"Shut the hell up, Danny. Be cool."

She gave me a quick kiss, and her lips felt like gooey plastic because of all the red-red lip gloss.

"You really do look beautiful, Abbey. Dangerously beautiful."

"What am I going to do with you? I want to make him jealous, okay? I just want to make him jealous. Now, are you satisfied?" She tugged on my shoulder. "Let's go."

We walked outside to sit on the porch with the others and wait for Domino.

*   *   *

"What the hell is this place? Some lost shack from Shanty Town? No, don't tell me, you guys are trying to start a commune, right?"

I looked over the porch railing and saw Domino for the first time, standing at the end of the trail leading from the main road to the cabin called Oz.

"Still full of compliments," Seth said. "What took you so long—you get lost?"

"Hey, donkey," Jay said, "didn't you remember all your forest shit from Boy Scouts?"

Domino smirked. "Seth-er, and Jay Wong, my main man. I came as fast as I could." He didn't seem to enjoy fielding ridicule as well as he enjoyed doling it out. "Boy oh boy, this place is mondo out in the boonies."

The girls remained seated, rather polite and stiff. I watched Abbey like a hawk.

"We call it Oz," Abbey said from her folding chair. "We happen to like living here a lot." She flashed a cordial smile. "We enjoy breathing air rather than smog."

"Well hello, Abbegail," Domino said. "It's been a long time, hasn't it?"

"Yes, yes," Abbey said, "a nice *long* time."

"And there's dear Cleo. Hey, pretty lady, what do you say?"

"Oh my," Zoe said, "hello, Domino." He rushed over and gave Zoe a bear hug.

Rather preoccupied with brushing off a spot of railing in order to sit without dirtying his fancy clothes, Domino said, "You must be the new drummer. What do you say, sport?"

"The name's Danny Vikker," I said. "I've heard a lot about you."

"Oh yeah? I haven't heard much about you." He laughed; I didn't. "Just kidding, sport."

Since the picture of Domino on the *Ivy League Drop-outs*

record cover was a cartoon, a water-color caricature, the image had provided only a starting point for my imagination. I had built Domino into a physical giant—a tall, dark, and handsome movie star—a beefcake boy, a Richard Gere, with a touch of Latino savvy.

Even worse, and more specific, I had taken to conjuring up terrible scenes of this magnanimous drummer on top of Abbey, his chiseled butt, their bodies squirming and writhing with hot, X-rated passion, screams of ecstasy in the air.

But now, not more than a few yards away from me on the front deck of the cabin called Oz, I saw a young man who was moderately handsome, well-dressed, yet big only by virtue of his commanding, arrogant repose. In stature, Domino was rather small.

He sat on our porch with his shoulders slung back like miniature cannons, his petite chest inflated, his voice compensatingly big and full of bullshit. He was rather like a puffer fish.

At regular intervals, his vision swam past Abbey; it was only then that his facade melted, and I saw something that looked like longing in the drummer's face. All the while, Abbey Butler sat next to me like a rock.

Domino reached over with his puny arm and gave Jay a good swat. "What do you do for surfing up here in Tahoe? I get out once in a while down south, but not like the old times. We used to do a lot of surfing in San Lu-E, didn't we, bud?"

"No shit," Jay said. "We did some tubing, dude." Both Jay and Domino climbed on the porch railing and pretended to surf. They crouched and laughed and exchanged Hawaiian lingo.

"Wiki wave, haole."

"Shaka mano."

They jumped down, both breathing excitedly. "You're looking real Hollywood, donkey," said Jay. "You must be making some major jack."

Domino wore a diamond stick earring, and jeweled rings on his fingers. His platinum blonde hair was gelled into place. He wore a black shirt with chrome rivets, black leather pants, and the most exotic-looking cowboy boots I'd ever seen.

"The P.D.s are taking the world by force. Hey, man, what can I say?"

"I know what you'd like to say," Seth said. "'Hey world, my name is Domino, and to you peons I'm a fuckin' king!'" Seth let out a half-hearted, polka-dotted party horn laugh. "Shit, just because you're famous doesn't mean you shouldn't act like a professional. You haven't changed, Domino. If you weren't so good, I'd have trouble taking you seriously."

Everyone laughed, not at Domino, not at Seth. Just to laugh. Most of the members of Bandit, it seemed, found Domino entertaining.

After a while, he said, "You don't say much, sport."

"Maybe you should call him Danny," Jay suggested.

"Shit, I like 'sport,'" chirped Seth.

"Whatever," I said.

"So, sport—. I mean Danny—. So you're the new drummer, eh? You and I are the ones that have something in common. Danny, my main man, you see playing drums is what makes it *click*. Other stuff—surfing for example—is just a cheap thrill compared to drums. *Comprehendo?*"

"You're pushing it, donkey. Surfing is a *click* with a capital 'C,'" said Jay.

"Yeah, and just as primal and animalistic as drumming," said Seth.

Domino pointed at Seth, indicating that Seth had amused him. "Anyways, sport, I consider myself lucky. I do what I love and get paid for it. So do you. Hey, I'm cutting albums and making a lot of jack. You're not. Hey, that's the way it goes. The point is: Drums are what makes it click for me—drums are my life-beat. Yeah, man, Dom's *life-beat.*"

Abbey and Zoe brought out a pitcher of wine coolers, and the mood became even lighter. Jay fired up a joint. I took a couple big drags to adjust my attitude, and passed the joint to Domino. "Don't do grass anymore," he said. He reached for his glass and took a dainty swallow.

"Getting religious?" Abbey asked.

"You know me, Abbegail, I want to be the greatest. Reefer is nice, but it messes up my coordination. I have my priorities. Drums come first."

Both he and she were playing it cool, but there was something about the way they looked at each other, as if there were knots in the backs of their eyes—knots that were taut and tense. It was what they didn't say or do that made me very uneasy.

*   *   *

It was Friday, noon. That night and the next we were booked at the Lone Star. That Labor Day weekend, the P.D.s were doing a three-night run, and Domino told us he'd get us V.I.P. passes for any night we wanted. Sunday, our night off, we would watch the P.D.'s grand finale.

Zoe grabbed some papers and a book entitled *Women Entrepreneurs: The Female Delight and the Male Plight* off the table and slipped them into her cordovan briefcase.

"Where you off to?" I asked.

"Here and there," she said. "I'm dropping by Caesars casino to work on getting us, possibly, a job in one of the cocktail lounges."

She asked for the keys to my truck.

"You sure you know how to drive a stick?"

"Seth's V.W. was a stick, and Abbey and I used to borrow it all the time."

"Be careful or you might run into Uwe," Abbey said. "He's such a pain, the way he and his friends have been coming to the Lone Star to watch us."

"We've only seen him there once or twice," I said.

"He and his buddies just like all the loose women at the Lone Star. I don't think they're interested in Bandit's music at all," Zoe said.

"Is that what he told you?" Abbey said.

"Relax," Zoe said. "He and his friends bought me one drink. One drink—let's not make a federal case out of it."

"There's nothing we can do about Uwe," I told Abbey. "Think of it this way—at least he isn't bothering us to let him back in the band."

"If you guys so much as let him sit in for one song, I'm quitting," she said.

"The worst thing we have to do is see his face once in a while, that's all. It's not the end of the world," I said.

"His awful face and his horrible pimples," Abbey said.

Zoe's recently plucked eyebrows became furrowed, her expression sheepish. She chewed nervously on the inside of her cheek.

"Oh my, I hate to antagonize you two, but don't you see? *He's* getting me in to see his boss about Bandit playing a cocktail show at Caesars," she said. "It's very difficult getting one's foot in the door at South Shore. Uwe's being extremely helpful."

"Why?"

"Maybe because he feels badly about making such a scene in S.L.O. I don't know. Does it matter?"

"God, I can't believe this," Abbey exclaimed.

"Don't you think I know he's a jerk, Abbey? Sometimes you think I'm so naive," Zoe said. "I'm just humoring him a little, that's all. He and I are having lunch today, and then he's introducing me to his boss. I'm just doing my job as a manager. It's all rather cut and dried."

"Is it?" Abbey said breezily.

"Yes!" Zoe said.

"Good God, why didn't you tell us about this in the first place?" I asked.

"I don't know," Zoe replied. "Because everyone hates his guts so much. Do you think I enjoy whoring myself, symbolically, as it were?"

"Don't you dare," Abbey said.

"I have no intention," Zoe said, seeming a bit pleased. "Don't worry. I have the whole thing planned out nicely. But, for now, we should all try to be nice to Uwe—until he's helped us out."

"The things we put ourselves through," Abbey said.

"Please let us know when the jig is up, so we can quit humoring the dumb lunk," I said.

"Don't waste a second," Abbey said.

*   *   *

Saturday morning, I awoke feeling glad it wasn't Sunday. Abbey was fooling around with some lyrics and Seth was accompanying her on his acoustic guitar. I drank a cup of coffee then walked to the pay phone on the edge of the cabin tract.

I called Sly's apartment to talk with Jay. I asked him if he wanted to go to the lake, maybe hook up with Eddy for some water skiing that afternoon.

"Sounds good, dude, but I already have something going on," he said matter-of-factly. "Me and Sly are meeting up with some of the P.D.s down at Sand Cove."

There was a pause. Jay's voice became more spirited. "Hey, why don't you join us? Bring Abbey, maybe Zoe and Seth—whoever you want. You could get better acquainted with my buddy, Dom, and the boys from L.A. They're totally off the wall, dude. You'd like 'em."

"Nah, on second thought, maybe I'll just stay around the cabin," I said. "Saturday night's always a big one at the Lone Star. I'm going to just keep a low profile and get ready for Mr. Clobber."

"Come on, man. You sound like an old lady. Come on, hit the lake with us."

Somewhere inside of me something cracked like a pipe and was leaking hot steam. "I got to go. Talk to you later."

"Come on, Danny. Come to Sand Cove. It will be a party."

The steamy heat inside of me made me feel more and more irritable. "We'll see. I'll cruise by later, maybe. I have things to do. So bye." I reached up and quickly depressed the switchhook. Jay's final sentence was cut in half: "Hey, man, are you jeal—." I regretted hanging up on him. The phone receiver was still cradled between my ear and shoulder; the buzz of the dial tone served as a strange penitence.

* * *

The statues were looking at me again.

As my eyes scanned the pre-concert milieu inside the Lake Club, I saw air the color of river water pouring through holes cut in sheet metal. It felt as though the blowtorch man and his friends knew me—and were assigned to watch me. What did those heaps of metal think I was going to do?

An impatient rumbling from the sell-out crowd coated everything. From our table on one of the best terraces, I saw rows of chairs set up on the dance floor in front of the stage— none of the chairs were vacant. I smelled the alfalfa-like odor of pot, and connected the smell to slouched bodies down below, secretly passing fireflies back and forth. Bouncers roamed the aisles, but they could no more stop these covert activities than stop a 200-ton avalanche. The pre-concert party had tremendous momentum.

Domino's drum set shined opulently like a prize display in a L.A. music store. It was a sea green Tama kit with double bass drums, a wide arc of tom-toms, and a panel of electronic pads over the hi-hat. Each cymbal was polished brassy-golden. The chrome rims and stands swam with blue, red, and green stage lights; like lava the lights swirled on his drums. Domino Gettsland meant business.

"P.D.! P.D.! P.D.!" Jay chanted along with the crowd. He sat next to us at a small cocktail table identical to the one Abbey, Seth, and I were sitting at. "Come on," he yelled at me, "get with the spirit. P.D.! P.D.! P.D.!"

Zoe, Eddy, and Uwe were sitting at the adjacent table with Jay.

"I can't believe he's sitting with them," Abbey whispered in my ear. "I mean, this is business. Bandit is here to watch another band for professional reasons."

"I agree," Seth said. "Inviting that clown, Eddy, was bad enough."

"Both of their names were on the guest list," I said, "written in black and white for crying out loud."

"She said she was going to get him in for helping her get us an audition at Caesars. But, God, he wasn't supposed to sit with our party. Domino got us these tables special."

"There's no getting rid of him now," I snapped. "SShhh. Live with it."

"Shit," Seth said.

Eddy checked to see if any bouncers were walking the catwalk, then I saw him pass Uwe a nose bullet filled with cocaine. Uwe helped himself to several snorts.

"I owe you one, buddy," I heard Uwe say to Eddy.

"You don't owe me anything," Eddy replied. "Have another. There's a good man." Eddy stood on his chair and yelled "P.D.! P.D.! P.D.!" at the top of his lungs. Eddy was smashed.

Jay laughed uncontrollably. He reached across their table and snatched the nose bullet from Uwe. Zoe put her finger to her lips and told the boys to shush.

There was a sheet of imaginary glass which prohibited conversation between our two tables. Abbey and Seth continued to say nasty things about Uwe, not seeming to care whether he heard or not. But Uwe was so busy chumming up to Eddy, and Zoe was so busy explaining to Jay about her new theory on how to win at craps, that the four of them were oblivious to the animosity. Zoe, Eddy, Jay, and Uwe were having more fun than I was. I felt stuck with sour grapes.

Sly came to the terrace and took our orders for drinks. "Make it quick, gang. The show is about to start. There's going to be a bloody riot in here tonight. The Pricey Dexters are just super," she said. Sly glanced around to see if any of the other cocktail waitresses were looking and gave Jay a wet kiss on the cheek.

"All right," Jay said proudly.

Uwe offered one side of his tanned but still pockmarked cheek to Sly. "What about me?"

"I'm a good girl," Sly said. "Only Jay gets my lovin'. It's not for just any gent."

Uwe turned to Zoe. "What about you? Will you give this poor boy a kiss?" he asked obnoxiously.

"No way, Uwe," Zoe said. "Why don't you calm down and mind your manners." Zoe was not inviting Uwe's attention, yet he was still a nuisance. He reminded me of a mangy dog, making messes with his slobber, his unsightly red thing hanging out.

"Mellow out, dude," Jay told Uwe. Uwe was hogging the nose bullet again, and Jay reached across the table to take it from him. Jay offered a snort to Sly. She refused because she was working.

When Sly returned with our orders, I heard Eddy ask Uwe, "What brings you to Tahoe?"

"I decided to bum around a little before I get serious and start studying again," Uwe said.

"College?"

"Law school."

Eddy nodded. "Do you like to ski?"

"Fuck yes, I can't wait until the snow falls."

"No, I mean water ski. I'd like to take you out sometime. Ask Jay, I have a great ship—the *Blue Max*."

"I like you Eddy. You have class. How'd you ever get to be friends with a group like this?"

Eddy smiled. "Jay told me you used to play in Bandit. Did you quit or something?"

"Yeah, it was time for me to move on. I have big plans for myself, understand?"

I watched him glare across the table at Jay and Zoe. Zoe looked away. Jay shrugged. "Cheers, dude," Jay said, gulping some beer. Uwe took a swig of his drink, too, and slammed down the glass. His laugh sounded more like a snarl.

A A A

"Hey teacher," I say to the bartender, "another straight gin on the rocks." He looks at me as if I'm some drunk slime ball. "Ah come on," I say, "I'm no Mario Andretti. I ain't driving. I'm with a whole bunch of great people."

Sour images of the friggin' great people spin by like some movie projector on rewind. The gin has a cold piny bite. It feels good on my throat, which is parched from the big roach Jay and I smoked outside on the dock after the show. Fuck it, I think. Fuck this shit. I slam down the rest of my drink.

"Hey, come on, teacher, I'm thirsty," I say. The round man who looks like he used to work in a barber shop gives me another. Skeptical, he makes it short. I shove it back at him and say, "Up to the rim. My money buys it up to the rim."

This bar is in a quiet finger that juts out one side of the Lake Club; the satellite bar is connected to the main floor by a sort of tunnel. I can see the big, blue lake and the private dock through panes of glass. The bar itself is against the windows, but the rows of bottles are kept down low so people can look out the friggin' view-window when they're sittin' here getting shit-faced like me.

Domino is such a good drummer that it embarrasses me. Deep down everyone is laughing at me because I suck eggs when compared to him. That's why Abbey and I had a fight.

"God he's awesome," she says to me. "He's gotten sssooo good. You know, Danny, you ought to try that beat, that lick, that solo.…"

The show gets over with, and I say, "Go on, run to him. I'll never be that good. Go on, run to that short sonofabitch."

"You asshole," she says, "I hate you." She's gone. Right then, she's out of there.

So I'm sitting here thinking about a couple other shitty experiences I've had, times when my friggin' ego got a rude kick right in the friggin' balls. The socks, maybe? Ha. Ha. Socks. Oh fuck, I hate myself.

Life can be the shits. Like in high school when I used to be so friggin' smart, a goddamn mentally gifted minor. Winning all those awards in math, entering school essay contests, joining the honor society, and all that bullshit. The ole parents thought I was a child prodigy or something. They bought me a new car and said I was bound for Stanford.

But the day of the SAT. Man oh man, I looked at that paper and went blank. Suddenly I was all tensed up, sweating. The questions weren't that hard. I just couldn't pick up my pencil and fill in the bubbles. When the results came, the old man was disgusted, thought I was a moron, said I didn't have the stuff. His advice was: "Don't bother to retake it. For love of Mary, go to a state school. What the hell is the matter with you, Daniel A. Vikker?"

Oh God. Or the time I got popped for drunk driving. Man, I kept that covered up pretty good. Just a few guys in my freshman dorm were the only ones that knew. Didn't seem fair, I drank just enough to get popped. One too many. That stupid beer party and those dumb, stuck-up chicks that made me squeal out of there and get loose in my car. Doing the public service was the worst part. Painting Avila Pier like I was some chain gang member, having to keep a low profile so that friends on the beach didn't recognize me.

This time. This friggin' time. All the humiliation comes from within. There's no one to tell me I'm stupid, no one to watch me. It's *just knowing Domino sounds five times better live than he does on his record. He's friggin' fancy, friggin' clean, friggin' FAST. It's so goddamn embarrassing thinking about all the times I've played with Jay and Abbey and Seth. I thought I sounded pretty good. But all along they knew my playing was a joke compared with Domino's. There's no comparison. No friggin' comparison. The whole idea of me playing in a band is a joke.*

I look out the window at the dark water. It laughs at me, too. Case Johnson strolls by—that arrogant sonofabitch manager. He tells the barkeeper to stop serving. What the hell does Case Johnson know? I'm so fucked up I don't think I can move off the stool.

I see Abbey walk out on the dock. I know it's her. I know her anywhere. Oh Abbey, I think, it's safe to watch you from here. Where's Zoe, I think. Or Jay or Seth. How come they're all not out on the dock talking about how much I suck?

It's like a friggin' Sunday afternoon movie. There's a moon out, a big piece of blue cheese. The moon reflects off Abbey's hair and makes a white patch on the top of her head. I love you so much, I think. Suddenly I think there might be a chance. "Get a friggin' camera," I say to the barkeeper who just told me to push off. "Look out the window at that girl on the dock. Isn't that some picture? You know I love that girl? I'll come right out and say it."

Ah, what a letdown. The little shrimp appears in the picture. Get out of there you friggin' shrimp. I just got a handle on my problem with you. She told me enough times it's over with you guys and I believe it; so get out of there shrimp. Domino walks to the end of the pier and stands next to her. Push him in, I think. This is funny. Push him in.

They're hugging. This is some trick, I think. Some friggin' optical illusion. I feel sick as he touches her. But I have to watch to find out about her side of it. I make myself watch.

They kiss and I watch his hands go all over her and hers go all over him. I start to cry. This is total evisceration, I think. I love her so much. My tears are hot and silent. They ride down my cheeks like they have wheels, pressing on my skin. Some turn the corner and spill into my mouth. I taste their salt. I press my lips together so tightly to keep the fluttering in my chest and throat from coming out my mouth that my nose runs. I don't want anyone to hear, to see, or to laugh.

The bartender asks, "Where's your friends, pal? We gotta get you out of here."

I can't face anybody. I stumble out a side door before he can come around the bar. The bartender does not follow. I have no coat. It's dark and cold outside. My face turns icy. I smell rotten garbage in my dark hideaway alley. I crouch next to a dumpster, intending to stay there until my guts have turned to stone.

A   A   A

After Domino and the Pricey Dexters played out their gig at the Lake Club and returned to L.A., Bandit's routine continued somewhat as it had before. We went on playing at the Lone Star, but grew increasingly tired of it. In time, the novelty of a place wears off—even a place with Mr. Clobber. Bandit's sights were locked on the casinos and, as ever, the Lake Club.

And what of Abbey and me?

I told her what I saw that night, and her response made me go limp. Like so many other aspects of her life, she said Domino was none of my business.

Our midnight rendezvous ceased; our conversations grew more and more polite and timid; and I continued to love her despite everything. Yet there was nothing I could do with our problem: we were prime numbers with no divisor. How could I persist without answers, in a relationship where one plus one doesn't equal two?

Abbey and I were sitting at opposite ends of the room ignoring each other, when Zoe and Seth entered the cabin, after having gone into Tahoe City on errands.

Jay got off the couch and helped them carry in some groceries.

"Thanks for letting me use your truck again, Danny," Zoe said. She threw me the keys.

"What's up, you two?"

"Nothing," I said, not looking at Abbey.

"Nothing at all," Abbey said, not looking at me.

"I have something for you," Zoe told her. She took a letter out of her briefcase. "I checked our P.O. box, and you received a letter from Izy's boyfriend."

"I can't wait to see what they're up to," said Abbey. "You know all the times you and I have gone to make calls lately. I don't know where on earth Izy's been the last couple of weeks."

"You know what I think?" Zoe offered. "I'll bet they're getting married."

"You know what I think?" Abbey replied. "I think you're right."

Both girls let out excited screams and Abbey tore open the letter. Abbey was much more happy now than she had been sitting around the cabin with me.

After reading the letter, she said nothing. Zoe kept saying, "Well? Well?" But Abbey didn't seem to hear her. The muscles that controlled her face quit functioning; her eyes became cold, wide ovals; her skin took pale; her beautiful mouth hung open like a wound.

The rest of us sat outside the door to the girls' bedroom, waiting, feeling helpless as we listened to Abbey and Zoe weep. The weeping of the two became the weeping of one, and Zoe solemnly joined us. Her face was swollen and red. When she tried to speak above a whisper, her words became chopped sobs; so she whispered to us: "Something awful happened. Izy and her boyfriend, Carmen, were in a car accident. A drunk hit them head-on. Carmen was lucky. Abbey's mother is dead."

Chapter 11
Hector

When the facts surface and, finally, one plus one equals two, wise men throw their Boolean algebra out the window....

Zoe and I were driving south from Lake Tahoe to Santa Barbara, when she finally told me the whole story about Abbey and Isabella Butler. With no abridgment of Zoe's insistence upon detail, and with all of her passion for events giving historical perspective, here is what Zoe Cleopatra Hash said:

A petite seven-pound, eleven-ounce baby girl was born March 21, 1960. If the little girl had been born one day earlier, she would have been a Pisces rather than an Aries. Astrology is terribly inexact, however. Abbey had acted like a Gemini ever since Zoe had known her.

Another significant point—at least as far as studious Zoe was concerned—was this: March 21, 1960, was the same day a man by the name of Jethrow R. Tunnelson patented the "Genohydraulific Link," a design for the primary mechanical linkage between a carrier vehicle and track in a bigger design, also Tunnelson's brainchild, for a state-wide mass transit system for California. Tunnelson's idea was ingenious. Later on, it ended up being cited in many socio-technological textbooks. But in 1960, his brilliant proposal for the "California Mass Transit" or "CMT," featuring the Genohydraulific Link, was shot down by a corporate board of directors. They said Tunnelson's proposal was unrealistic and unpractical—one director even went so far as to call Tunnelson and his CMT, "a ludicrous dog 'n' pony show." Several years henceforth, Tunnelson died of a heart attack. Twenty-one years later, it was too late for a lot of people like Isabella. Everyone—including drunks—continued to drive their smog-bellowing automobiles everywhere. Oh my.

"Abbey Irene Butler" hadn't been sixty seconds out of the womb, before the head obstetrician at U. C. Berkeley Medical Center said two things one right after the other, which Isabella Butler would never forget: "I've never heard a more delightful little cry.... I've never seen a newborn with such devilishly cute eyes...."

Abbey lay on her mother's stomach; a funny audience of elves dressed in surgical garb encircled mother and newborn child. When little Abbey started to wail, it was as deafening as the sound of cracking ice, but the small crowd around Isabella and her new daughter didn't seem to mind. There was something magical about the tiny girl's twinkling, tear-filled eyes that made the doctors and nurses stand at fond attention.

Young Isabella was full of ethereal happiness as she swaddled her child in the recovery room. Motherhood suddenly felt right to her, and it seemed her life had taken a turn for the best. Actually seeing her baby—actually touching, smelling, and hugging the warm rubbery flesh—was wonderfully reassuring. Although Izy was an optimist, and found much solace in her music, art, and in her passion for the Society Pages of the *Los Angeles Times*, up until that point, her existence had been all but charmed.

When Isabella left her hometown of Kalamazoo, Michigan, to attend University of California, Berkeley, the Cool-daddy-O Fifties were in full swing and about to collide with the Tune-in-Turn-on-Drop-out Sixties, and young Izy, who was sick of her parents—and their droning television, cigarettes, and emphysemic coughing—willed herself to become a raving beatnik/musician. She was tired of life being dull.

Her first two years at Berkeley, Izy tried drugs, the next step beyond heavy petting, and various other forms of madcap adventure, all for the first time. Izy was popular around campus because she was pretty, and could sing and play the guitar. She wrote her own songs and sang them on the steps of the Administration Building. She could also play the piano and the violin, even better than she played the guitar, but those instruments weren't in at the time.

Unfortunately, the girls in Izy's college dormitory became jealous of Izy's popularity and started a rumor that she had gonorrhea. There was a V.D. scare going around campus at the time.

"She's a tramp," the dorm girls said in the halls as they passed by Izy.

The young men in the dorms were nicer than the girls to Izy's face, yet behind closed doors, the boys' meanness exceeded the girls'. "Izy's got a scabby cunt! Izy's got a scabby cunt!" they chanted like football players breaking a huddle. And the walls in the dorm were very thin.

For the record, Izy did not have gonorrhea. Yes, some dorm girls did see her at a free clinic, but she was there only because she had a yeast infection and didn't have enough money to be treated privately. Oh my.

But Izy was a survivor. Her junior year in college, she got a job at a small dinner club playing piano, and she moved off-campus into an apartment. More and more, she fell in love with her musical studies. Her professors at Berkeley greatly encouraged her. They told her that when she applied herself she was a virtuosa.

Then, one night at work, Izy met Ethan Chamberlin. He was handsome, worldly, and very complimentary of Izy's piano playing. Since leaving the dorms, Izy had been lonely, and she found Mr. Chamberlin's affections flattering. They went to a play the next night and consequently shacked up in Izy's small studio apartment.

There were several things Izy didn't know about dashing Mr. Chamberlin: (1) his real name was Jeff something, (2) he acted suave and sophisticated because he'd found this to be an effective guise for getting pretentious young skirts into bed, and (3) he was an Army clerk on two weeks furlough from a military base somewhere in Arizona.

Jeff something, a.k.a. Ethan Chamberlin, left no address when he returned to Arizona. Izy never saw him again. He also left her pregnant.

Isabella's mother, Irene, died of lung cancer during Izy's first trimester of pregnancy. Her father, Jack, died the year before from the same disease. Shortly before Isabella Butler received her bachelor's degree, she gave birth to the by-product of her torrid, deceptive affair with Mr. Chamberlin. Wary of beaus and cigarettes, yet truly pleased and content with her baby daughter, Izy proceeded on with graduate work at Berkeley and received her Ph.D. in music when Abbey was four years old.

From then on, Abbey Irene Butler grew up in Santa Barbara, where her mother first taught at University of California, Santa Barbara until—because of lack of sincere appreciation from her students, her colleagues, and the community in general—Isabella concluded that folk and classical music made a better hobby than a career. She began making candles and lost faith in higher education.

According to what Isabella had managed to tell Zoe (Abbey, it seemed, disliked for her mother to talk about her childhood), Abbey was the type of little girl who loved to wear her mother's clothes, and, since Isabella was lenient, also her mother's makeup.

Abbey was precocious and preferred the company of adults; she went with her mother everywhere. Clomping behind Isabella in size seven high heel pumps, little Abbey was evidently a cute spectacle—with red rouge smeared on her cheeks and forehead, an assortment of jeweled combs in her long brown hair, and a string of her mother's lovebeads dragging on the ground.

In grade school, Abbey had a vocabulary twice that of any of the other students, yet her marks were poor. During parent-teacher conferences, Abbey's instructors often told Isabella about how Abbey wasn't working up to her potential.

"She's just a child," Izy liked to retort. "Why pressure her?" It was a mind game Izy confided, if the teachers would have responded with intelligent answers, she would have been happy to listen. But the teachers would merely parrot the rules.

Abbey actually liked this part of her childhood story, and adored her mother's superior attitude toward public education. Zoe related how Abbey sometimes chimed into her mother's reminiscences in a lofty, baritone voice:

"Our educational standards are based upon national averages for varying intellectual student-competencies," they'd say. "It concerns us that Abbegail's performance always lands on the left side of the bell-shaped curve, even though her I.Q. presents scores well above normal."

"So what you're telling me," Mother would say, "is that you don't like her getting 'C's' and 'D's' because some silly index, based on her I.Q. and national statistics, says she should be getting 'A's' and 'B's.'"

"Exactly, Mrs. Butler," they'd say. "We're so glad you understand."

"Fiddlesticks!" was Mother's reply to that horseshit!

Oh my.

Anyway, Izy had a unique conception for Abbey's education. As far as Isabella was concerned, if one knew how to play a musical instrument, and read and write, one was adequately prepared to brave the world. She wanted her daughter to be a survivor like her, rather than someone obsessed with getting "A's," "gold stars," and "happy faces" on their homework.

Abbey grew to be a free-spirited teenager, although she

continued to love her mother and home life. After school—that is, when her mother didn't write her a note and Abbey had to actually go to school—Abbey helped Izy at her leather shop, or she studied her music and read gossip columns and racy novels. Abbey proclaimed that she and her mother were best friends. She felt that she could talk to her mother about anything, and, since she was as precocious a teenager as she was a child, she did.

Around most of the other teenagers, Abbey looked different because she preferred to dress like famous singers she saw in the rock 'n' roll tabloids—rather than like a Barbie doll or cheerleader. The regular kids bored Abbey, and the few kids that looked like her were too rough for her tastes; so Abbey did her own thing. She joined a local band of older kids who dropped out of the university to play rock 'n' roll.

Abbey's first band, Katrina's Taxi, developed a big name around town fast. Especially popular was the group's dynamic teenage songstress. Around Izy and her artist friends, Abbey was witty and outspoken, yet around other people, for most of her life, Abbey had been quiet and subdued. Onstage singing with Katrina's Taxi, Abbey Butler opened up to the world. She discovered that holding an audience in the palm of her hand was her niche.

She also discovered that she could employ her flamboyant onstage persona offstage as well, and, with that, she became a young woman who had a reputation for being wild and bizarre. Izy was fully aware of the coming-of-age of her daughter and approved of the new Abbey, all except for Abbey's cigarettes. Izy's disapproval of her daughter's one vice was subtle. When Abbey smoked, her mother would call her by her middle name, Irene, the name of Izy's deceased mother.

"Stop it, mother," Abbey would retort. "Oh stop it, Izy."

Oh my.

Abbey was seventeen and graduating from high school

when Katrina's Taxi broke up. Much to her teachers' dismay, Abbey graduated in the top half of her class. Isabella had done her job: Abbey was a survivor and could read, write, and play a musical instrument, which was more than most kids.

Despite Isabella's cynicism toward college, she suggested that her daughter "go to college to experience its pleasures and pitfalls." So Abbey moved to San Luis Obispo and enrolled in the state college there as an English major; what she really had in mind was to join another band. Her first couple of months away from home were horrible. She was homesick and trapped; she had no car; even if she did have a car, she didn't know how to drive one, since both Abbey and her mother thought cars were obnoxious.

For a couple of quarters Abbey was a good student getting "A's" and "B's." As far as she was concerned, she didn't have anything better to do. Abbey and her equally studious roommate, Zoe, quickly grew bored of the dorms and moved into an apartment. Abbey had never had many friends her own age and tended, according to Zoe, to be rather bossy, as if she were Zoe's mother; even so, the two became inseparable, going to numerous parties and drinking and smoking pot and getting smashed. Zoe maintained her grades; Abbey quit going to her classes.

At one of these parties, Abbey met Domino Gettsland, who said that he had once heard Abbey sing in Santa Barbara. He asked her to join a newly formed band called Bandit. Domino Gettsland was even bossier and wilder than Abbey, and she didn't like him at first. But she did want to start singing again.

Bandit—with Abbey, Domino, Seth Collins, Jay Wong, and Uwe Vladt—was an even bigger success than Abbey's first band. Bandit landed gigs at all the local clubs and played Santa Barbara and Ventura County as well. There was talk of a small, local recording studio doing an album. Domino and Seth, however, convinced the rest of the band to wait until they had further progressed with their originals. "When we're ready to make a break," Seth, the guitarist, told everybody, "let's make a BIG one."

For some reason that was unknown to Abbey, she fell in love with Domino, and in the beginning she felt their relationship was just about as star-studded and flashy as any rock 'n' roll couple she'd ever read about in the tabloids. Things went splendidly until one month when Abbey misplaced her birth control pills. Soon after that she recognized that she was pregnant.

There was only one solution as far as Domino was concerned: abortion. Domino told Abbey he refused to be a father. "I care for you, Abbegail," he said, "but, man oh man, a kid would really get in the way."

Domino had ambitious plans. He wanted to get his degree in music, then return to L.A., where he would join with some of his old music buddies who were equally as talented and ambitious as he was. His paramount obsession was to make it bigtime in a rock 'n' roll band. To him, San Luis Obispo was an educational vacation. S.L.O. was much too smalltime for a permanent residence or career.

In Abbey's mind there was only one solution also: having the child. She couldn't imagine abortion. After all, she was an illegitimate child herself. But Domino had made himself perfectly clear.

Only Domino, Zoe, and Abbey knew about the pregnancy. The rest of the band figured Abbey's sour, depressive mood would pass, like it always did when she over-indulged and became sick with a hangover. Before she began to show with child, she shocked the band and its fans when she announced she was quitting Bandit to move back home to Santa Barbara. Domino was relieved to get rid of her. It was the saddest day of Zoe's life.

When Abbey arrived back home in Santa Barbara, Izy

assured her that she had made the right decision, and vowed that mother and daughter would get through this thing together.

Abbey occasionally spoke with Zoe on the phone, but other than that, she cut herself off completely from San Luis Obispo. Bandit continued to play. Domino never really admitted to himself that Abbey had their baby. He chose to believe a rather terse, flip letter from his ex-girlfriend. The letter read something like this: "In case you're interested, I didn't have the abortion, but there's no need to get yourself into a tizzy. I had a miscarriage. Isn't that convenient? So please, Dom, don't bother to give me any more sympathy for all my problems. That would be sssooo uncalled for. You jerk, I don't ever want to see you or Bandit again...."

An eight-pound, thirteen-ounce baby boy named "Hector Butler" was born on Ground Hog's Day, February 2, 1979. He received an overabundance of love from both Abbey and Isabella, but at his first routine checkup, the doctor discovered the baby boy would grow up to be retarded.

Abbey and her mother took the bad news well, as they were both survivors. But it was sad all the same. Hector had Minkinson's Disease, a rare condition resulting in minimal higher cognitive functioning due to underdevelopment of the frontal lobes of the brain. To put it simply, Hector would grow old without learning how to read, write, or play a musical instrument. Hector would not be a survivor. Someone would always have to look after him.

Zoe finished relating all this information around the time we turned off Interstate 5 onto Road 41 heading toward Paso Robles and the coast. After mulling it all over for a while, I said to Zoe, "One thing is for sure. It all adds up very nicely. A lot of things make sense that didn't before."

"One plus one certainly equals two," she replied.

It was hot and dry outside, and, though it was October, the

coastal foothills were still scorched brown from the summer months.

The unseasonal heat gave my voice a lazy edge, "No more guessing. No more And/Or logic. It's friggin' time to throw the ole Boolean Algebra out the window."

"That's the understatement of the year," she said.

The vinyl seats in my truck were uncomfortable in the heat. She bent forward to give her back some air. Her blouse was damp, and the outline of her bra strap raised the shear fabric. A whiff of her moist skin whisked past me and blew out the window; her sweat smelled like pollen from a fresh flower.

"I was just thinking."

"What?"

"It's nothing really."

"Oh my, don't you know the line: 'Only fools keep their thoughts at bay.'"

"Yes."

"Really, Danny."

"I was just thinking," I repeated, "what would it have been like if you and I got together, instead of Abbey and me."

She smiled demurely. "You're awfully sweet, Danny. But you're not my type."

I had to laugh. "You're not really my type, either," I said. "It's just that sometimes I wonder why."

"That's an easy one to answer," she said. "You're too much of an absolutist at heart. You fail to see that reality is subjective. I'm a humanist. I believe that our values, our laws, our history, our future, our *situations*, none of these are cut and dried. You're sweet, but a bit tilted, Danny. Most of the time one plus one *doesn't* equal two. Do you see?"

"You read that in a book?"

"I've gleaned portions of it from many books and put it all together." She gazed out the truck window at the dry brown grass on the hills. Still looking away, she said softly, "No matter what happens, Danny. It's okay to love her. She's sweet, but a bit tilted, too. Oh my, it's okay."

None of us had heard from Abbey since we left her at the Tahoe City Greyhound Bus Station three weeks before. She told us she didn't want any company on her trip to take care of things for her mother. Abbey had been brief in describing her immediate, as well as future, plans. We didn't know if she was coming back.

In the meantime, Zoe had finally gotten Bandit another audition at the Lake Club, and we were not ready to do it without Abbey. Perhaps it was selfish—we needed our rock 'n' roll diva to fulfill the band's destiny—but the rest of us had talked about it—we felt Abbey needed us, too.

Zoe and I were headed to Santa Barbara to tell Abbey this.

* * *

We stopped in San Luis Obispo for a cold beer before continuing on to Santa Barbara and ran into Spook and his roommates.

My eyes locked on Spook the minute I walked into Aces; after all, he was the only person in the place wearing a top hat and a black pullover with a glow-in-the-dark skeleton painted on it. It also appeared that he had shaved his head; pink scalp shined beneath the rim of this top hat. Good ole Spook, I thought, you've gone further off the deep end.

For what seemed like a long time, he stared cautiously at Zoe and me, before starting toward our table. Behind him, he pulled a whip-like strand of leather, which was fastened to a plastic model of Godzilla. The green monster stood on a homemade wooden platform with wheels. Godzilla's head came nearly to Spook's waist. As the mobile beast rolled behind Spook, its wheels hummed like an insidious Tonka toy.

Spook took off his top hat awkwardly; he sort of curtsied rather than bowed; the top of his head was equally as pink and shiny as the sides. "Do you remember Jane and Leslie?" he said, acknowledging the two girls at the rear of the parade.

Bird-like Jane and saucy "Flipper"—both girls noticeably drunk—plopped themselves into a couple vacant chairs. Spook carefully put his top hat back on and sat himself properly, then attempted to roll Godzilla underneath our table. The monster didn't fit, and Spook had to bend the monster forward on its stiff, socketed hips.

"I can take his head off," he told us, "but I always have trouble getting it back on." He glanced under the table. "I don't really like to bend him, either. His joints get loose."

"Why'd you put him underneath the table anyway?" I said. "Good God, he's very entertaining."

Spook's expression was bland. "The bartender already warned me once before. He says the fire marshal doesn't allow monsters on carts to block the aisles. Personally, I think Aces is prejudiced."

"Hummm," I said.

Zoe searched for something to say, "Tell us, Spook. What is your monster's name?" Her tone of voice sounded more appropriate for a business lunch than drinks with Spook and company.

"His name is 'Ken,'" Spook said.

"Isn't that a cute name for a lizard?" Flipper said.

"He takes Ken everywhere," chirped Jane. "Even to class." She was still thin and pretty. I smiled at her, and she angled her blue bird eyes away.

"To class? Oh my," Zoe said. "That's rather a breach in academic protocol, isn't it?"

"Maybe. It won't go on forever. It's my and Ken's last year…and then I'm leaving."

"Really?" I said.

"Yes, I'm going to medical school, just like I planned," Spook replied.

"He's getting a full scholarship from Stanford," said Flipper. "All he's got to do is cruise through a couple more quarters."

Spook proudly rolled Godzilla out from under the table. "Ken has become my mascot, my good luck charm," he said. "Ken helps me to keep straight and studious."

"And what does Stanford think of Ken?" Zoe asked.

"Of course they've never seen him," Spook said. "Do you think I'm hhoorrrrr-ribly weird?" He showed a sliver of yellowish teeth. "Do you think doctors must conform to a certain stereotype?"

I certainly did, but I kept quiet.

"Oh my, I hope you don't intend to be a pediatrician. You would frighten the little kids and give them nightmares," Zoe said.

"To confess," Spook said, "I want to become an expert on organ transplants."

"Isn't that gross?" Jane said.

"He wants to be a Dr. Frankenstein," Flipper said. She held up her beer mug and some beer sloshed out of the mug onto the table. "Here's to the Doctor," she said.

Zoe sat in silent disbelief and unconsciously rubbed the side of her neck, as though she feared that she, herself, might be making a nightmarish transformation and neck-plugs were beginning to push through her skin.

We finally got around to talking about Bandit, and we passed on the bad news about Abbey's mother but said nothing of Hector. Zoe had already made it clear to me that it was up to Abbey to expose Hector to the outside world, if she wanted to.

Good ole Spook was sympathetic of Abbey's plight and extremely complimentary of Bandit's success in Tahoe. He promised to come watch us play the Lake Club if we got the gig.

I wasn't sure if Tahoe was ready for Spook. I wished I had a camera to take a picture of him and his monster, Ken. It would make a nice photograph for my father. "Here's your goddamn man around Stanford," I'd write on the back. "P.S.—Medical School, top of his class."

The more I thought about it, Isabella Butler was right. The most important things were the basics—to read, write, and play a musical instrument. Since I had graduated from Cal Poly and gone into the world, I hadn't come across one—not one—practical situation where I required Boolean Algebra, Laplace Transforms, Differentials, or Vectors in Three-Space. I knew significantly more than I needed to know to be a survivor. I should have been more than prosperous and content. I had all my answers: one plus one equalled two. But I didn't have Abbey Butler, did I?

*　　*　　*

When people die there is first grief, then resolution, followed by fond memories and decisions about what to do with their stuff.

My freshman year I, like most students, lived in the dorms, and my roommate was a nice, unassuming kid by the name of John McDonald. John had the strong, wholesome build of a farm boy. He wore glasses, had furry eyebrows, and always seemed relaxed. Another distinguishing characteristic was his dark, closely cropped hair which he shampooed once every three days and kept styled wetly with hair tonic.

While many of my fellow dormies had problems adjusting to their roommates, I never had a problem with John. He was predictable, getting up each morning precisely at 6:45, and leaving for campus after breakfast at 8:00, where he spent all day at class and the library. He returned for dinner at 5:00, where after he would occupy his small desk in our room and do more homework or read his latest issue of *Sportsman* magazine. I, unlike John, exhibited freshman behavior that was closer to the norm, and my life followed no set pattern, but those evenings when I remained in my dorm room, John and I often had nice talks. He would tell me about his courses or sometimes about his life back home in Utah. I would sometimes tell him about problems I had with my dad, and he would listen empathetically and say nothing. Each night John was in bed by 10:00, and he slept like a rock and didn't snore.

Monday through Friday John treated his school work just as though it were a job and kept right on top of his studies. On Saturdays and Sundays he also rose at 6:45 A.M., although there was a variation in his routine. On Saturdays he went on outings with the Cal Poly San Luis Obispo Sportsman's Club to hunt, rock climb, canoe, or do whatever rustic activity that was planned. On Saturday nights he had a steady date with his girlfriend, Jill, who was nice and unassuming like John. Jill always wore loud, bright colors, and had a hefty rump and a thin upper lip which never seemed to cover her gumline. Jill didn't know how to handle a smart remark and clammed up if you kidded around with her; when she dropped by our room to visit John, she and I didn't talk much. On Saturday nights John and Jill went western dancing; on Sundays they went to church.

I sometimes remarked to fellow dormies that John and I were about as similar as oil and water, and whomever I was talking with would always say something to the effect of: "Yeah, John gets all his oil from his hair. Hah. Hah." Though everybody liked John—especially me.

One weeknight I was procrastinating in my dorm room. I had an awful calculus test the next day and didn't understand the last three homework assignments one iota. John was cleaning his hunting rifle, a lever action 30.30, and I found this activity exceedingly more interesting than calculus.

"Going shooting around here?" I asked.

"Club's sponsoring a hunt this Saturday. We're going to see if we can get a boar."

"No shit?" I exclaimed. He looked at me mindfully;

profanity was offensive to John. "I mean, *no kidding?* Get a boar?"

"There's a bunch of them in the coastal hills—domestics that have gotten loose and gone back to the wild." John checked the lever action on his rifle. "Give pigs a free rein and in a couple generations they'll grow back their bristles, and the boars will take on tusks."

Talking with John about his club's pig hunting expedition and watching him work on his gun made it easy for me to continue to neglect studying for my calculus test.

After a while he said, "Come along if you like as my guest. I can get you a gun." That was the first time he asked me to go on one of his club outings, and I felt badly turning him down. But pigs? The thought of being confronted by a pack of them in the wild was too scary. I told John no thanks and said I would be eager to hear all about the hunt when he got back.

But that was the last time I saw John McDonald. His funeral was closed casket because there wasn't much left of his head after being shot accidentally by one of his fellow sportsmen. Evidently, John's group hiked several hours in the hills before spotting a herd of wild pigs. John and a few of the more ambitious sportsmen charged the game. One of John's buddies who remained in the flank sighted in a pig on the scope of his deer rifle, and, just as he pulled the trigger, John's head popped up and centered itself in the middle of the scope's crosshatches. Bang. John McDonald was dead.

It was a week or two before John's parents came around to pick up his stuff. One of the hardest parts of dealing with the experience of losing my roommate was coming to grips with the things he left behind. His personal items stirred me most. His toothbrush lay neatly on top of his dresser, in the same place he always kept it, on the right alongside of a three-quarters-empty bottle of Vitalis hair tonic. When I looked at these things—the toothbrush with John's dried saliva on the bristles, the bottle of hair tonic with its outer label sopping with shiny oil like John's hair—I felt the presence of death more vividly than I had ever felt it before. I wanted to clear his dresser and desk, to take down his calendar with his important dates off the wall. I wanted to de-humanize his half of the room, so that I didn't have to think about him anymore.

But I couldn't bring myself to touch anything of John's; his belongings remained poised in place defiantly, frozen animals waiting for their master to come home.

Until John's folks came and boxed up all of his things, I avoided my room, and when I had to go in there, John's toothbrush, hair tonic, books, and clothes stared at me. I would sit on my bed, with my back against the wall and stare back, thinking about John and what his voice used to sound like.

*   *   *

Just as I had to deal with John McDonald's personal effects, Abbey had to deal with Isabella's, and this plight, I realized, was ten-fold more traumatic, since Izy had been Abbey's mother—her only living family besides her son.

"What do you think I ought to do with this place?" she asked Zoe. "Izy's rented this apartment for years. It's where she raised me." I witnessed much strength in her as she sorted through her mother's affairs, yet her whitewashed, zestless tone of voice was a constant reminder that her composure was painfully forced.

The two girls finished dispensing with Isabella's personal things in the master bedroom. The last of Izy's hair combs, cosmetics, and dresser-top knickknacks went into a cardboard box with "Sun-ripened California Oranges" printed in black and orange letters on the outside. Zoe held the flaps while Abbey sealed the top with a wide strip of tape.

"There," Abbey said, "I just couldn't stand looking at that stuff another minute." She lit a cigarette, took a puff, and sighed. "Zoe, dear, you didn't answer. What on earth am I going to do with this place?"

"Carmen said he'd look after the shop until you've made a decision about that. That's one problem solved," Zoe replied. "If you plan to stay in Santa Barbara, I think you should keep it. Your mother was very proud of this place. Personally, I love the view."

"It would feel very strange to live here without her."

"Well, of course, we'd love to have you come back with us."

"Don't rush me," Abbey said. "Please, Zoe." She shut her eyes and took deep breaths. "I know you guys want me back," she said. "This is sssooo hard."

"I didn't mean to needle," Zoe said.

"I know," Abbey said.

Zoe went to her spiritual sister and gave her a hug. "Oh my, I wish this whole thing never happened. It's terrible. If only we could go back in time."

Emotion overcame Abbey, and her eyes blistered with tears. "I miss her so much. God, Zoe, I miss her." Abbey managed to stop crying for a minute, and, seeming embarrassed, she glanced at me. Her cheeks were stained with streaks of mascara. She began to sob again.

Little Hector, who was sitting on my knee, had no idea what was going on. Kids with Minkinson's disease, Abbey explained, weren't able to comprehend sadness. He was fascinated with the big cardboard cube that his mother and her friend had been playing with. "Gop? Gop? Gop?" he said for about the hundredth time.

"Come to Ab-gy," his mother called. "Come on, honey. We're done in here."

I felt Hector squirm; so I plunked him down on the floor and he crawled to his mom.

Abbey grabbed him like a sack of rice, and she and Zoe strolled out of the room. I trailed behind, stopping at the doorway. Izy's bedroom was now faceless like accommodations in a motel. Yet there was something invisible, ominous and haunting, that lingered in the air of the room. Poisonous, yet scentless, formaldehyde.

Abbey put Hector down for his nap in the other bedroom, the room which the girls had kept secret when I visited here before.

Large fixtures of Izy's life remained in the living room. Abbey and Zoe sat together on the bench seat of the baby grand; beside them, Izy's old violin and guitar slept in their wicker basket. Zoe folded her hands in her lap; Abbey's fingers caressed the ebony and ivory keys, transmitting a coded melody to felt hammers inside the baby grand; when the felt hammers hit the strings, a passage of notes stopped time.

An Oriental blue, vase-like vessel rested on top of the piano, and Abbey's eyes regarded it fondly. She talked in a low voice as she played; she wasn't singing; her words followed the notes like a dreamy lover follows a butterfly:

"Ashes, Mother, all that's left of your body are ashes. You and I, we talked about dying. You said if anything ever happened—and I never thought anything would happen—to please not put you underground, where it's dark, where it's cold, all wrapped in awful silk ruffles. You believed in the spirit, Mother, not the body. Throw me into the wind, off the Golden Gate, you said. That would be nice. Powder the wind with me, you said and laughed, away with my ashes and then, daughter, away with yourself. Abbey, you said, I'd do the same for you...."

*   *   *

Abbey Butler decided to return with us to Lake Tahoe; for how long she didn't know. It was cramped in my truck, and little Hector had to sit on Abbey's lap. He chortled and drooled and messed his diapers, and Abbey hugged him and nuzzled his curly brown hair. We journeyed first to San Francisco and walked to the middle of the iron-orange bridge spanning the entrance of the bay. Solemnly, Abbey dumped the contents of the blue urn over the edge of the bridge—into a gusty breeze, which would carry the ashes toward the gray Pacific; some of the ashes floating further, perhaps, on the wings of salt air, till they reached the shore—to rest under a green shrub, to meld with shells on the dirt and sand. When the urn was empty, Abbey threw it off the Golden Gate as well.

Chapter 12
Playing Solidly

The heavy snows still hadn't come, but the shorter days and weak yellow sun told us fall had bid farewell and winter had arrived. There was a lull in the tourist trade, and the clubs weren't as crowded. Soon white flakes would coat the mountains for winter sport, and snow skiers would converge upon the Sierras. It was a crazy time of year for us to be at Sand Cove.

Our beach party consisted of Bandit, little Hector, Sly, Eddy, Tish, and one of Tishy's friends. The Cove's gently sloping, granite-sand beach was otherwise vacant. Much to everyone else's dismay, that idiot, Eddy, had taken the liberty of inviting Bandit's ex-keyboardist to the party; Uwe was supposed to arrive later when he got off work. Eddy had somehow gotten chummy with Uwe, or vice versa, after the two of them met when the P.D.s played the Lake Club. Jay and I hardly ever got to go boating anymore, because Eddy was busy with Uwe. I guess it didn't matter too much; water ski season was over.

* * *

The late afternoon sky was a pretty azure blue and perfectly cloudless; yet the flawless atmospheric ceiling didn't match the brisk wind whistling past our frozen ears; the wind was a bully, and greedily consumed what little heat the thin, glass pipes of crystalline winter sunlight carried down to the earth. Jay was the only person who was shirtless; he insisted that the sun, although heatless, still had enough ultraviolet power to tan, but even Jay stuck close to our raging bonfire.

"Whiskey," Jay said. "Pass me the bottle, dude." I handed him the quart bottle of cheap liquor that tasted like rotten wood. The clear, medium-brown liquid was almost gone; what remained sloshed in the bottle. No one seemed to give a damn about starting the barbecue.

"You know what?" I said. "You look like a friggin' Indian with your shirt off and all. Aren't you freezing your ass off?" The whiskey made me feel weird and edgy. I felt an urge to scream at the top of my lungs—to run like a mad dog into the big, blue lake. But it was too friggin' cold.

"Fuck you, Vikker," Jay replied.

"Fuck you, Wong-dong," I said.

"Well fuck, fuck, fuck," Jay yelled like a maniac. We laughed until our eyes watered, bobbing and swaying on our whiskey legs, as though we were a couple of marker buoys floating on the choppy lake.

Abbey, Zoe, and little Hector sat on a smooth, gray driftwood log a cozy distance from the bonfire. Even though the wind was shifty, it always seemed to blow the smoke away from them and in the direction of somebody else. The girls were not so inebriated as some of us and didn't mix in with our rude conversation; instead, they held a private, sisterly pow-wow. Abbey had bundled Hector up so completely that he looked like a puffy, quilted ball; the hood of his jacket was drawn tightly around his head, and his face was chopped off around the edges, as though it were mounted in a picture frame that was too small. Occasionally, one of the loud, sloppy young adults would try to get his attention: "Hey, Hector. Hey, hey, hey! What's ya doin' down there?" But the strange, unfamiliar people amped-out his mind; he issued no reaction. He remained quietly in a daze, with his mouth drooping open and his hand clamped tightly onto his mother's. The little guy's lips looked like grape Popsicles.

There was no sunset at dusk; it just got dark, and colder.

Seth went to fetch his guitar. Abbey followed him carrying little Hector. I heard Seth stumble in the darkness and yell, "Shit." When he returned to the bonfire, he was alone.

I hiked to Jay's van and heard the engine idling. I shuddered with pleasure when I slipped inside; the heater was on full-blast.

"Hi," I said. "Maybe we should move the party in here? Good God, this feels nice."

Sitting with her back against the carpeted van compartment, Abbey stroked the fine, curly brown hair on top of her son's now unbundled head; her caresses hypnotized the tiny boy. "Actually," she said, "I was enjoying the solitude."

"I'll drive you back to the cabin, if you want," I said. "Who knows when this party will end. Everyone's just getting started."

"Don't worry about us. Hector and I will be fine," she replied. "I thought we should get warm for a while. I don't want him catching a cold. It could cause complications—with his condition, I mean."

"Want some company?"

"No, that's okay. When dinner is ready, come get us, will you? Bye, Danny."

I returned to the party solo and suggested that we break out another bottle of rotgut. I was thirsty for another friggin' drink.

Looking like a bawdy minstrel, Seth stood in the bonfire's orange floodlight and played his guitar. When he finished the song, he thumped the body of his acoustic and said, "Make a request somebody. Shit."

"Play a fuckin' protest song, *donkey*. Something rowdy," Jay suggested. He hung onto Sly as though she were a lamp post.

Sly was more sober than her boyfriend, yet full of spirit herself. "Play another bloody song whatever it is, gent. Doesn't matter, does it now? Play, Seth. Bloody play!"

Becoming more engrossed with listening rather than balancing, Eddy tripped on the sand and fell face-first into it.

"Man, did you guys see that?" Jay bellowed. "Eddy, dude,

Eddy, that's the funniest thing I ever seen in the whole wide world!" Jay stumbled, too, and fell down next to Eddy. Laughing and laughing, the rest of us who were standing let our knees buckle, and we collapsed on the beach. We wallowed in the cold, gritty sand and made pockets to lounge in.

Seth let out a polka-dotted party horn laugh. He rose, and shook the sand out of his guitar, and began to strum and sing a favorite tune by the Stones:

> *If I could stick my hand in my heart,*
> *Spill it all over the stage,*
> *Would it satisfy you?*
> *Would it slide on by you?*
> *Would you think the boy is strange?*
> *Ain't it a stray-yeh-ange?*
>
> *If I could win,*
> *If I could sing,*
> *A love song so divine,*
> *Would it be enough for your cheatin' heart*
> *If I broke down and cried.*
> *If I cry-yi-yi'd.*
>
> *I know*
> *It's only Rock 'n' Roll,*
> *But I like it.*
> *I know*
> *It's only Rock 'n' Roll,*
> *But I like it, like it,*
> *Yes I do—*

The crackle of the bonfire replaced the sound of Seth's scratchy voice and melodic guitar. A broken guitar string curled off the guitar's neck. Seth hadn't brought any spares.

Eddy decided that a spin in the *Blue Max* might clear his groggy head. Most everyone wanted to go with him, even though it was dark outside. I stayed behind to cook the hamburgers and hotdogs. We needed to get some food in us. I searched for the utensils, grill, and cooler in the sand.

Down at the water's edge, Eddy powered-up his boat and switched on red, blue, and white lights. The *Blue Max* looked like a carnival ride. The boat cut a neon wake as it rocketed into the darkness; I listened to the wake backlash against the shore. The rowdy cheering onboard faded. Last of all, I heard Jay yell: "Fuckin' bon voyage…."

A girl appeared at the fire.

"Boo," Tishy said, wrinkling her nose. "Need any help?"

"Sure, maybe," I said. "Good God, you scared me."

"Burr, it's cold. *Ooooh. Ooooh.* It feels so good to snuggle." She pressed against me and latched onto my arm. Sluggishly, I bent over the coals and formed the corners of a square with four hefty rocks. I put on the grill, but one of the rocks wasn't big enough; so I used a flat stone as a shim. I asked Tish where her friend was.

"She's barfing," Tish replied matter-of-factly.

"Is she going to be okay?"

"She'll be okay," Tish said. "It's no big 'D.' Let her barf. She'll be ready for more later. She's hardcore."

That night Tish was wearing a rather exciting outfit underneath her nylon ski parka—a skin-tight jumpsuit with a chrome zipper from the neck to crotch. She didn't appear to have on any underwear. One part of me said: pounce. Another part of me said: dodge and parry. This time, I listened to the latter, to the voice of my good fairy. The hamburgers and hotdogs sizzled on the grill.

"Uwe should be here soon," Tish said, bored with watching me cook.

"You know him, too?" I said.

"He's such a clod. He owes Eddy about $600 for coke, but Eddy doesn't make him pay because Uwe kisses his butt and makes excuses. I think my brother's kind of afraid of him."

"Does Uwe ever say anything about us?"

"You kicked him out, right? I heard him tell Eddy that."

"That's not exactly what happened."

"Who cares?" Tish said. "I swear he's *so* ugly. When he tries to come on to me——. It's like, totally gross."

"Maybe he won't be able to find his way here in the dark," I said.

"The less people the better. I'll bet the *Blue Max* won't be back for a while. You and I should lie down together. *Ooooh*, it's so cold."

"Don't get too comfortable. What about your friend? How long do you expect her to blow chowder?"

"You're not as fun as you used to be."

I gave her a friendly pat on the rear, happy, actually, for the chance to cop a quick feel. "I'm sorry," I said.

Tish swung her wonderful little behind toward me again and batted her eyes. "Do it again, Danny. Tee-Hee. Harder!"

That's precisely when Abbey appeared and wanted to know how the barbecue was going.

We ate when the rest of the gang returned from their post-sunset boat ride. Somehow sand had gotten into everything.

Gritty hotdogs, hamburgers, and buns. Gritty ketchup and mustard. More whiskey. Burnt marshmallows. More shouting and wallowing in the sand. No end in sight.

Abbey needed to get Hector to the cabin; so I shuttled them back to Oz. I tried to explain that Tish and I were just kidding around.

"I don't give a hoot about you and that little bitch. I know you screwed her. She tells everyone."

"That was before——"

"I don't care."

"Yes you do."

"No I don't."

She placed her hand on my shoulder and squeezed firmly, without affection. "For the time being, you and I have no strings attached, remember? I have to get things sorted out. Go on and have a little roll with Tishy. That's your problem."

I turned onto the dirt road near our cabin. Hector was fast asleep in his mother's arms.

I parked the van. Before Abbey started along the trail to the cabin, she moved her hand through a bunch of dark pine needles on a low, bushy branch. "I told Domino about Hector."

I said nothing.

"He's coming to hear us play at the Lake Club. He and I are back together, and I want him to meet his son."

It was late, but what the hell. I drove back to Sand Cove.

"Welcome," Uwe exclaimed when I reunited with the gang. "You made it. I'm thrilled."

"Likewise, I'm so honored to get to party with you bozos."

He was hogging the whiskey bottle, trying to catch up with the rest of the drunks. He wore dress slacks and a necktie underneath his jacket.

"I like your monkey suit. Just get out of your cage?"

He frowned, then turned and yelled to Zoe, "Hey, baby, I told you to come over here. Come and see your old friend, Uwe. Don't be shy, honey-child!"

Zoe was stumbling around in the darkness from person to person, checking up on everyone as if she were a party hostess or something. Zoe Cleopatra Hash was ripped. I probably should have taken her home with Abbey.

Uwe put his greasy face next to my ear. "Hey, Vikker, what do you think my chances are for getting Zoe wet between the legs?"

"You're sick, donkey," I said. "She's got way too much class for you."

Zoe wandered over. "Hello, boys. How are you doing? Oh my, someone's got to make the rounds. Are you having a good time? I am. Oh my, let's see, how are your drinks?" She put her arms around each of us and kissed our cheeks. She burst into a Bandit original—singing horribly off key.

"Why don't you let me take you home. This party's a dud," I said.

"Oh my, have another drink, Danny. Just because Abbey left, you aren't going to be a spoilsport, are you?"

Uwe snorted.

"Very funny," I said. I pulled Zoe away from Uwe, who was fondling her back with his big, dopey hand. Uwe sailed over to flirt with Tish and her little friend, who seemed okay now, except that her breath smelled atrocious.

Uwe didn't have much luck with Tish, and I watched him walk over to Eddy. The two clowns grabbed the last bottle of whiskey and headed to the waterline. "Hey, crew," Eddy yelled, "last call. Who wants to go on a midnight cruise?"

No one responded. It seemed like it was getting about five degrees colder every second; the bonfire was the place to be.

"Come on," Eddy persisted, "I'll make it a short one."

Zoe buttoned the top button on her jacket. "Oh my, what the heck," she said. "I'll go." She ran down to the *Blue Max*. The rest of us stayed behind.

I rubbed my hands together in front of the fire. The lights on Eddy's boat drew an arc in the darkness, toward the entrance of Emerald Bay.

Some of us grew sober; some of us did not. Seth lay passed out alongside the coals of the bonfire; he snored loudly. Tish's friend was barfing again; so was Tish. Jay lay in the granite-sand like a corpse with his arms crossed X-fashion over his chest; Sly mumbled at his sleepy face. I sat on the piece of driftwood which the girls and Hector had occupied earlier on. My mind roamed through memories of me and Abbey. The fire slowly died.

Quite a bit later, Jay propped himself up on his elbows and said groggily, "Where the hell are those guys? We oughta split. The ranger's gonna come or something."

Eddy, Uwe, and Zoe had been gone for at least an hour. Get your boat back here, Eddy, I thought. Damn.

We waited. We froze.

The *Blue Max* returned at approximately 1:30 A.M. Three silhouettes, even blacker than the night, stood in the boat as the bow rode up onto the sand. The engine quit, and the search-light and running lights popped off.

Zoe stormed out of the darkness biting her lip—her hair looked windblown, and her scarf was wound around her neck like a Band-Aid; there were so many turns that no end hung down.

"I want to go back to the cabin," she said to me. "I want to go back NOW." Her voice was sober and blank. Her eyes aimed sideways to avoid looking at me dead-on.

Eddy and Uwe walked up from the shoreline. Eddy seemed nervous. Uwe was in a hurry.

"I gotta split," Uwe said. He kept walking toward the parking lot.

"Hold on," I said. "What's going on?"

Uwe didn't turn around. He started to run.

Jay caught Uwe and held him by the collar of his jacket. He kicked Jay in the leg, but Jay hung on. "Tell me, dude," Jay said, more soberly than he'd said anything all that day and all that night, "what the fuck's going on?"

Zoe stood frozen. "What's up?" I asked. "Were these guys being jerks, or what?"

Eddy fell to his knees in the sand, as though there was a tremendous pressure which caused him to whither. "I didn't do nothing. I swear. Nothing," he said. "I was all messed up. I just held her."

Jay grabbed a handful of Uwe's hair. "Hey, dude, what's up?

Cough it up." Sly latched onto Uwe's jacket. Uwe spit in her face.

I collared Eddy. I shook the hell out of him. "Did what, Eddy? Did what?"

"You don't have to tell them anything," Uwe said. "She's not going to tell them anything, either. It's our secret. I made her promise."

"Did what?" I repeated.

"Nothing," Uwe barked. He tried to wrestle free from Jay and Sly, but they held fast.

Eddy started sobbing. "We were both just kidding around at first. You know, to scare her or something. Uwe screwed her, man."

"Ah shit." I pushed Eddy's face into the sand. I felt like kicking him, but something inside stopped me. I threw up my hands and went to Zoe.

Uwe screamed wildly, "I should have done it to Abbey. Zoe was the next best thing. You guys fucked me. So I had to fuck you back." He broke loose and punched the side of Jay's head. Jay staggered, then surged. He grabbed another handful of Uwe's hair, this time forcing Uwe to his knees.

"You sonofabitch," I yelled at Uwe.

Uwe spit on Jay's leg. He laughed. "You bunch of losers. Fuck you. Fuck all of you. She has a nice cunt, did everyone know that? Real nice."

That was the only time I ever saw Jay Wong completely lose his cool. "Shut your dirty, low down mouth, dude." He bunched together his fist and slammed it into Uwe's face. I was standing nearby, and the impact was sick and hollow, like the sound of a dog or cat being hit by a car. Drops of what, at first, I thought were rain, appeared on the tops of my hands; examining them closer, I discovered they were droplets of blood.

*   *   *

"What a pair, sport. What a pair," Domino said, regarding the two girls with a long glance.

"Yep," I said, "what a pair." Him calling me "sport" still bugged the hell out of me.

We sat in the Lake Club in a terrace overlooking the stage. In the chair beside me, Domino glistened. He wore a silky white suit with aqua-green stripes, and gray shark skin boots. The boots gave the friggin' shrimp some altitude, I thought smugly. The bangs of his long, blonde hair were trimmed perfectly straight; a thick application of hairspray held every strand in place.

"Don't worry about getting upstaged tonight, sport. It's been suggested that I sit in for a song or two. Boy oh boy, wouldn't I love to? But I've decided to keep a low profile tonight and give you all the glory. Think you can handle the responsibility, sport?" His expression displayed shades of arrogance, camaraderie, sympathy, and compassion—layer upon layer of plastic, enigmatic, Hollywood bullshit. "Just remember to keep it simple and steady up there, sport," he added. "You'll probably do okay."

On the stage below us, Abbey and Zoe fussed with the setup, making sure the instruments and amps were plugged in, working, and perfectly arranged. Normally the girls didn't have anything to do with this menial duty, but this was not a normal gig. Seth Collins was also fiddling with our equipment, but then, Seth always did that. The girls kept having to straddle Seth as he scooted along the stage floor on his hands and knees, ducking under keyboards and dodging amps while he searched for loose cords to secure; Seth had bought a brand new roll of silver duct tape for Bandit's Lake Club debut. Zoe pointed to Abbey's electric piano, then drew some sort of diagram in the air; the girls attacked the slim but weighty instrument, and, with much exasperation, relocated the piano a foot or two from where it had been.

Still looking down at the girls and Seth, Domino said,

"People are funny, aren't they, sport? They're kind of like rubber bands. They snap back, you follow? Take old Cleo for instance, boy oh boy, all the crap she's been through—and she's down there joking around." He nodded his head philosophically.

It was my turn to intimidate.

Science. Numbers and equations, that was my turf—when one plus one equals two.

"People are resilient—just like a rubber band, as you put it—only to a point," I replied. "Sometimes you can pull a person past their elastic limit. Hooke's Law, then, no longer applies. Do you understand the concept of non-linear stress versus strain?

"Furthermore," I continued, "this rubber band you speak of is inside a person. Therefore, when it breaks, sometimes the person doesn't know it. An external observer—like you or me—is even worse equipped to detect a broken rubber band. Good God, we don't have X-ray eyes, do we?"

I was very pleased with myself. Your move, Domino.

Domino merely ignored what I said.

"Cleo's a tough kid. That much is obvious, sport," he said reflectively. "Even so, I'd love to get my hands on that Jerk-ola, Uwe. I never did like him. He's a shitty musician, and he has a bad attitude. He's a loser, man."

The haunting scene played again in my mind.

Uwe lay crumbled and motionless after Jay had busted open his face. No one tended to him, and no one hurt him anymore. Eddy kept crawling around in the sand like a big baby. Everyone kept telling Eddy to shut up.

Jay's rubber band had stung him when it snapped, and Jay got mean; he didn't strike Eddy like he'd struck Uwe, but each time Eddy tried to cower up to the people standing around Zoe, Jay chased Eddy off. Eddy finally got the message when Jay kicked a bunch of hot coals from the bonfire at him.

Zoe's rubber band didn't snap; it disintegrated. We stood around her in the eerie darkness as she cried. She couldn't seem to wrap enough blankets around herself. Her weeping was the kind of weeping that hurts to have to listen to. It made me start to cry, too. And Zoe's painful crying made all of us—including Tish—kick at least one dollop of sand onto Eddy, whimpering several yards away in his cold, gritty purgatory. Uwe lay unconscious.

The days immediately following the incident at Sand Cove had been tough on Zoe, too. Zoe was a lot like Abbey in the way she tried to act brave and tough when the chips were down. But she couldn't hide it; the people in the cabin called Oz knew she was badly injured inside. She gutted out the days; when the door to her and Abbey's bedroom closed at night, the crying began. It was soft, muffled crying. At night Zoe let her pain leak out, not all at once, but steadily like air spilling forth from a pinhole in a tire.

Zoe was a virgin before Uwe came along. Not many girls, these days, are still chaste at age twenty-one. Zoe knew this. That's why she kept it private.

She had been waiting for true love, just as a lot of the women did in Zoe's history books. That summer and fall, the new Zoe Cleopatra Hash got closer to the point of finding Mr. Right; she hadn't seen him, but she sensed that he was near. Zoe was independent; she loved to make plans; she loved for her dreams to come true. Uwe Valdt messed up everything.

And then, there was the business of Uwe disappearing. We had thought he was out cold when we left him to take Zoe to the van. Seth drove Zoe home to Abbey and Hector, and Jay and I returned to the waterfront to mop up Uwe and take him to the cops. Instead of Uwe, we found Eddy sprawled in the darkness. Tish was screaming at him, "You wimp. You spineless wimp. I'm embarrassed to have you for a brother."

Tish turned to Jay and me. "You're too late," she said. "That sneak, Uwe, wasn't as bad off as you guys thought. He just let my brother have it. I guess I should thank you guys for coming.

He was about to hit me."

Jay and I watched the lights from the *Blue Max* disappear out on the lake. We didn't see or hear from Uwe again. The cops couldn't find him, either. Zoe decided not to file charges against Eddy. I thought she should have.

Domino was baby-sitting Hector, as he and I sat in the Lake Club in a terrace behind chrome chain-link fence. No more talk of rubber bands. Our conversation grew sparse.

Little Hector wasn't any trouble at all. He sat on his father's lap, preoccupied with a baby bottle full of Coca-Cola. Hector sucked on the bottle with the slow cadence of a resting heart, making the sound: *ba-glurp, ba-glurp, ba-glurp.*

Domino held his son with cool authority; occasionally he addressed him, saying things that tended to indicate something temporary about their arrangement. "There's your mom down there. See her? Boy oh boy, she'll be back real soon."

When Abbey cared for Hector, she became enthused about every utterance and every movement the kid made. He was prime entertainment for her—but a dull fact of life for Domino.

"So tell me. How is it to be a father?" I asked.

Domino patted Hector on the head, then stared penetratingly at me. "Let me be honest with you, sport," he said. "In some ways this thing with Abbey, me, and the kid is a kick. In other ways it's a plot." The drummer's gray-blue eyes swept down to the stage and the girl, and remained focused on her. "I really do love her, and I suppose I ought to marry her. That's what you really want to know, isn't it, sport? So that, my friend, is what I'm telling you."

*   *   *

The beat I played was a simple one, eighth notes with the bass drum on *one* and *three*, interspersed with quarter note rim shots on the snare drum on beats *two* and *four*. (1& 2 3& 4.) Thud-thud-Swack, thud-thud-Swack. We were playing our

most popular original slow tune—a ballad, the music written by
Seth, the lyrics by Abbey. It was called "Mr. In-Question."

I could float on this big, blue lake
Forever — thinking of you.
Red roses, red candles, red tears.
Oh dream-boy, why must I always run ahead
Looking back, dodging years?

It's me Mr. In-Question, ain't you.
It's this pain I have. Gotta
Hide it, save it, brave it.
It's not enough for me to lay down for you.
I'm twisted fire, you see, no one's chick.

Sorry Romeo that fate's so damned.
I think of ways to make it better,
Money, I think, or Big Bang — What, man?

It's question after question, Mr. In-Question.
Lover, I just can't give ya my passion.

I pretended that Abbey Butler's voice was my one-person
audience, as I played my drums. I felt patriotic. I saluted the voice
and the song's sweet irony by playing as solidly as I possibly
could. Deep, loving concentration. Pure, precise movements.

Thud-thud-swack. Thud-thud-swack.

The harder I beat on my drums, the more satisfaction they
gave back, satisfaction like a person feels when you pound on a
thick oak door and the wood makes a tenor-humming, satisfaction like hitting a tennis ball in the sweet spot of the racket so
that the ball sails low and fast and the racket sings. In the pocket,
in the groove, playing solidly—that was where it was at.

Drummers like Russ Kunkel and Ringo Starr were kings of

the solid, laid-back beat. They made it sound easy, but it's not. Playing solidly: just going through the motions isn't good enough, it's an exact science. The beat can't push; the beat can't drag. Each note has to be dead-on-the-number, a twin with the note that came before—in pitch, in volume. When you play a fast song, what you do as well as how you do it becomes important; during a fast tune a drummer's allowed more flare, freedom, syncopation, and dazzle. Once in a while you can even forget the bass line and go off on a tangent. But on a slow song, the drummer has to keep it laid-back; he's got to hit hard and right on the money. The beat's the pedestal, and it's got to be precise and made out of dark-blue iron.

Thud-thud-swack. Thud-thud-swack.

What I tried to do was lay down a beat for "Mr. In-Question" that would last a million years.

Caged behind a fence of tom-toms, mikes on chrome booms, and brassy cymbals, I peered at slow dancers. The song's romantic charm glazed the dancers' eyes; my big, solid beat skewered each dancing couple, and turned them vertically, about themselves on a merciful, bloodless rotisserie.

Thud-thud-swack. Thud-thud-swack.

The inside of the Lake Club was very familiar. Statues with nothingness eyes. The smell of cigarettes and humans. A poster picture of a dark matrix of fool's gold, neon, pockets of infrared, always New Year's or Christmas. Hot sex sizzling. Forlorn drunks. Liquor bottles filled with *juice*.

Thud-thud-swack. Thud-thud-swack.

There. Up on the terrace. Those people were old friends, even Domino sitting with Hector on his lap.

Good ole Spook, looking more reasonable than I ever saw him. No top hat. No chains. No rubber spider. No plastic Godzilla named Ken. Very mild appearing, in fact, in his Levi's and *Rocky Horror Picture Show* T-shirt.

"The metamorphosis has begun," Spook told me before the

show. "Stanford University is a different scene."

"You're melting, Spook," I said.

"I'm melting. I'm melting. How could you do this to me, Dorothy?" Spook chanted.

"You know, Spook, I'm glad you showed up," I told him. "You're a true patron."

Melvin Stevenson, Jr., a.k.a. "Spook," smiled shyly.

After the show that night I would find something and be strangely touched. There would be a large cardboard box in the cab of my pickup. In the box I would find a Godzilla doll named Ken. Symbols are funny, aren't they?

Thud-thud-swack. Thud-thud-swack.

Next to Spook sat Zoe, our manager, mooning fondly and carefully down at her band. She still glowed with innocence.

Thud-thud-swack. Thud-thud-swack.

I couldn't look at Domino and Hector again.

Thud-thud-swack. Thud-thud-swack.

I saw: the backs of two young men, whom I felt strong bonds toward. Jay Wong and Seth Collins faced the audience and played their guitars like rock 'n' roll knights. When I looked past Jay and Seth into a pool of bodies and faces, I caught a glimpse of Sly, bustling energetically, from table to table.

Thud-thud-swack. Thud-thud-swack.

The song consumed itself, and Abbey turned around and prepared to give me the ending cue. Bandit left the ending of "Mr. In-Question" loose; Abbey repeated the last line as a chorus until the moment was right:

> *I'll never know, Mr. In-Question*
> *yea-aaaah*
> *I'll never know, Mr. In-Question*
> *yea-aaaah*
> *I'll never know, Mr. In-Question*
> *yea-aaaah....*

As she double-checked to make sure she had my attention, her expression was bedazzled and remote; she was beautifully enslaved by her own song. Green eyes, brown hair, mouth painted red. Boots, sassy, bra-less. Witchy aura, youthful artist, magic flower. Abbey Butler.

Thud-thud-swack. Thud-thud-swack.

She winked, spun around, and, with a clenched fist, punched the nightclub sky. While solidly, just as solidly as I possibly could, I struck two small crash cymbals—one with my right hand, one with my left. Instead of quickly reaching up and clamping off the sizzling metal dishes to effect a clean STOP, I let 'em ring.